Chasing The Rift

By: Kathy Roberts
Copyright 2017 Kathy Roberts

Cover Art by:
Author Laura Wright LaRoche
www.LLPIx.com or LLPix Designs.

Chasing The Rift

by Kathy Roberts Copyright © 2017.

All rights reserved.

No part of this publication may be reproduced, stored in a retrieval system or transmitted in any way by any means, electronic, mechanical, photocopy, recording or otherwise without the prior permission of the author except as provided by USA copyright law. The unauthorized reproduction or infringement without monetary gain, is investigated by the FBI and is punishable by fines and federal imprisonment.

This novel is a work of fiction. Names, descriptions, entities, and incidents included in the story are products of the author's imagination. Any resemblance to actual persons, events, and entities is entirely coincidental.

Cover Design by: Author Laura Wright LaRoche
Contact her at: www.LLPIx.com or LLPix Designs.

For Breanna, always.

Do what makes you happy in life, but never forget your responsibility to help others and always strive to leave this world a better place than you found it.

If you can, make a change that will benefit others; but never make it at the cost of others.

Mommy

First and foremost, always, I want to thank God for everything and everyone I have in this life and all that's in store for me in the next.

Without Tammy Sovine and Christie Edmunds, I would be lost in a sea of typos, misspellings, various gramatical errors and continunity issues. You are the best and I can never thank you enough for all you do in supporting my work. Love you both!

Also a special thank you to all my friends and fans who support me through buying my books, giving me words of encouragement, getting excited about my books, and telling others about what I do.

Chapter 1

Come in Tom. I'm getting pretty anxious to hear what you've accomplished since we last met. That was a pretty big list you had to check off. Have a seat and fill me in on all the details.

Hey Mike, it is good to see you. If you'll grab me an iced tea, I'll start. I guess the biggest news is I did secure the federal grant that tags onto the NASA grant. I've got the responses from the twelve prospects at West Virginia University. I'd like you to help me go over them and choose. Then I'll schedule interviews and get an up close look at them. I want at least six, but may start with eight as I'm not sure how long they'll last. The internship requirements have listed the need for course completion of and 4.0 average grades in the advanced courses of Optics, Physics, Electricity, Magnetism and quantum mechanics. I also stressed weight, strength, and physical requirements of this project. I alerted them to the fact that our accommodations are extremely primitive as well as there are no communications that work in the area. They will have no idea where they're going ahead of time so nothing can be leaked to the press. I have NASA recommendations for Laurel Fork Federal Wilderness in West Virginia, to be our location for the base camp, set-up and experiments. I've already secured the best physician available, Myra Livingston. She's about as excited over the whole thing as I am. The seclusion, mountains, and extreme terrain should keep out onlookers and keep in the energy we'll be using. I have nuclear, atomic, tachyon, magnetic and laser energy sources available, so we can't have anyone very close and we need the mountains to hold it in as well. Could you imagine loosing that kind of energy in a wide open space like Montana or the Great Plains? It could wipe out everything within a thousand miles. We may as well just eliminate the US if that happened. I think the mountains will absorb a lot of what we're using. NASA is providing the food, tents, some new technology in bug control-- especially mosquitos, all the various power supplies, transportation and helicopter drops to the site to help us get there faster as much of the terrain would take days to traverse. Oh, I'm working on one last guy's approval to get plutonium as well. They really want this technology and if we can get it started, they can develop and finish it. I can feel it Mike, we're on the brink of time distortion, or shifting, or travel even. We just have to work the equations and do the trials to see which source works best. We've done too many studies and hypotheses for it not too. If we can accomplish what I think we can, we may not be able to reverse history, but we can definitely stop wars and major mistakes from happening in the future. If we can travel back, forward, or even repeat as much as six hours of time, it would be unthinkable the disasters we could avoid; the lives we could save and disastrous decisions could be fixed or eliminated for good. Now let's get started.

Tell me a little more about this location first.

It's tucked between long narrow ridges in the heart of the Allegheny Mountains. It is one of the most inaccessible areas of West Virginia and is primitive backcountry. They are the least visited place in the

919,000-acre Monongahela National Forest. There is fresh water from cold mountain streams and enough forestry to hide us from prying eyes and overhead observations. They have a primitive campground between the two areas with sixteen spots. We won't be using them, but we've rented them for the entire season to eliminate anyone coming in to camp. Camping is not allowed outside the campground area, so hopefully we won't be bothered.

Sounds perfect, but be careful to secure plenty of water should any of your experiments contaminate the water supply. Now let's get started with picking through the students we, I mean you, want. Sorry Tom, I'm just so excited. If only I were thirty years younger, I'd be going with you.

I understand and I'd want you there. First is **Denver Johnson**, he's an excellent scholar with a 4.32 GPA from high school through graduate school. He excels at everything he attempts. He's designed two new fuel cells that NASA has implemented for the space shuttles. They are called the Johnson Cells and are a derivative of plutonium and very stable. He has a couple of his own theories on time travel and we'll be testing them both as we conduct my trials and your theories'. He's on their short list of recruits and he wants it badly too. He's physically fit and a survivalist, so he would be extremely useful should we run out of food, have a medical emergency, water issues or whatever may happen. He has done extensive experiments with magnetic and laser energy as well. As far as I'm concerned he's exactly the kind we want, it's just a matter of locking him in and since NASA is a major player, I think we've got him already. Now we move along to **Margaret Williams,** my second choice. She believes everyone should be physically fit and goes on survival trips with Denver all the time. I know she could carry her own in the rugged terrain and in the tough conditions. She is a quantum physics guru. I'd venture to say she knows as much on the subject as any human on the planet. She just built the latest bomb for our military. She calls it the quantum cocktail. Apparently she's used atomic and hydrogen energy together to create a super destructive force that doesn't do the damage to the land and infrastructure like the atom bomb.   Third choice for me is **Alan Swann**. He's an excellent student, hasn't missed a day of school since he started kindergarten, he's volunteered for every extra lab, every internship, every teacher's assistant position there has been. His IQ is 160. He's basically off the charts. He is mathematically versed and has all the qualities I could ask for in a quantum physicist, but the boy is severely lacking in common sense. I really think this will help him with that. I don't think he would be dangerous to us, he's not that bad, but I think he needs some survival and directional skills. He's been so engrossed in his thoughts and projects that he's gotten lost. He was literally five miles from his starting point when he looked up. He truly needs to lighten up a little bit and I don't ever recommend that to anyone, well at least until now. My fourth candidate is **George Duncan**. George is a jock. He loves sports and plays a mean game of football, but he loves power even more. Anything that generates, or amplifies power is on his list of most favorite things to do. Because of his love of sports, he is great with people. He will be the team leader and they will all get along because he's the glue and it will work because he has as much knowledge as they do so he won't just be trying to look like something he's not. He actually has the highest GPA of them all at 4.69 and he's quite the ladies man too. I think that's more of a distraction for him, so he can let his mind rest and refresh. He understands recharging the old brain power. Next up is **Alison Davis**. She is another super genius and her field of home study is tachyon pulses. She's been doing experiments at home; she even built her own emitter. My only issue with her is she's made a couple statements about global peace. I like the idea myself, but it won't just come because everyone believes we should just play nice. It comes from hard work, politics and who's got the biggest gun. You know that's right. Our hope is to change that balance some too. I just hope she's not too radical. Hopefully we'll be able to tell in our one-on-one interviews. I do think this can be a quality we need in our group; someone to help everyone pull together and no one get a superiority complex. My last candidate for first string is **Steven Henderson**. He is obsessed with particles, their mechanics, bodies, how they react to various energies and inertia, how they can be manipulated, etc. He'll be our guy to monitor any physical changes or attributes of the team as we're the ones involved directly in the experiments should they expand to include us as they're progressing to full power. He's a perfectionist and demands order in every experiment. He'll be the guy to check and double check everything to avoid accidents. I like that too.

Tom, I think you've got all the bases covered for the type of people you need and you definitely have the brain power to manage controlled experiments. I think you've considered the human elements of these people too and how they'll complement each other and interact as a team. You've honed in on their strengths and weaknesses, so you know up front what you'll need to address. You've done a good job my friend. Now to the alternates or additions you may choose to make.

That would be **Ryan Holly**. He's a data freak. He's constantly adding to notes, jotting down times and dates of things. I think he would be a great asset to avoid missing anything should we need to recreate an experiment. He's 99.9999999999999% accurate on every project or experiment he's been involved with. Computers aren't quite that accurate. I've met him; he's a really nice guy too. He'll work well with the others and he's physically fit as well, so no issues there. Oh and he has an amazing camera setup, so he'll take pictures of everything and everybody. Now last but not least I want **Jody Frame**. He's extremely obsessed with inertia, energy momentum and the effects on immovable objects. I think he will be our environmentalist here. We don't want to destroy the wilderness; we want it to help us contain our energies. He's a hands on guy; he likes to work on cars, and rebuilds engines. If you ever get the chance to buy one for your car, do it. He gets 275 horsepower and 43 miles to the gallon in a full size sedan. He's going to revolutionize the auto industry if they don't get rid of him first with some scandal. Big oil money takes care of their own you know. He's a loner, but can be a team player too. Now if you'll look over the last four applications and see if you can find anyone in there any better or better suited than these, let me know. I'm going to fix me some more tea while you do that.

Help yourself. I'll get right to these. You know where everything is if you want a sandwich or anything else. I find these students extremely interesting. Do they already do projects together? I notice some have the same experiments listed as others. I think you may already have a team with some great back-ups in line should one get sick or something. I believe they are exactly what you need for accomplishing this time portal. Is that what you're going to call it? The weather may be a factor, have you considered that as well? I didn't notice any of them having any meteorological training, do you have someone else in mind for that or just going on the knowledge you have and hoping that's enough?

Thanks for the sandwich and tea, did you want anything? (Mike shook his head) OK. I think George has had a couple classes in it, just because he was curious and was studying wind patterns for another experiment he was working on, so with the two of us, I'm hoping that's enough. Yes, they have worked together, not the whole team, but a couple or three on different projects. That's another reason these eight are my top picks. I haven't decided yet, if it works, it will be Silvers Time Slicer, I think. Is that Sci-Fi enough for the skeptics? I'll decide very quickly though, if it's a complete success. If it partially works, I'm not sure. I guess it depends on what works and how effectively it works. I just hope we have enough time and energy for the testing of all the theories I have worked out and those we come up with on the spot. I do think this group is on the cutting edge of anything relating to time, power and dispersion of each. Mike, I'm like a little kid getting ready for his birthday party or Christmas. I am nearly giddy. I've worked for this and waited so long, I can hardly believe it's actually about to happen. I'm calling the students today to set up the one on one interviews. I hope they're all available tomorrow so we can get the ball rolling as quickly as possible.

Tom, I'm truly happy for you and it has been a pleasure helping you with what I could and watching you become a great scientist. I have the utmost faith and confidence in you. You will succeed, I just know it. Anything at all I can do from here on out, just let me know, I'll do all I can.

Thanks Mike, you've been an amazing inspiration to me as well as mentoring me through every step of my career. You'll never know what all that means to me. If I were a woman, I just might cry. (When they finally stopped laughing, Tom continued.) I thought we could both use a good laugh and I haven't laughed that hard in years. I have tears coming out of my eyes.

Well you'd better wipe them away quick before I think you are a woman! (again the laughter) See I got a turn at making us laugh too. Seriously though, I am proud of you.

Thanks again. Well I've got to run, lots to do.

They shook hands, gave each other a punch and a manly hug and Tom left with the biggest smile on his face ever.

Chapter 2

He was able to set up the face to face interviews the next day with the eight chosen students. Just as expected they were all excited and every question he asked them was answered and just as he'd expected as well. He liked them all and had a good rapport with them. He'd asked each in turn if they could choose a team of eight, who would they choose. There were only a couple of them who chose a different person than one on the team. He then revealed his list of top contenders and, in turn, they all gave their approval and was confident they could all work together and would make a great team.

He told each one as the interview was over that he'd call them the next day and advise if they were on the team or not and he'd send lists that night of what he wanted them to bring and what the limits would be for their personal belongings they could bring. He explained it was a tight schedule so they'd need to get started gathering their stuff once they knew for sure.

After the last interview Tom knew he'd chosen well and this team would work well together. Now to wait till morning to call them all and let them know they've been chosen and give them the pick-up location, date and time of their departure. They only had two weeks before it all began.

Myra

Tom, it's so good to hear from you. I'm so excited. I know we're going to do amazing things in West

Virginia. I've already packed my bags. I was just waiting for the date, time, and pick-up location. I think I've gotten all the specific supplies you asked for, but if you think of anything else, be sure to let me know. When you have the medical history on the students, please e-mail them to me right away so I can make sure I have necessary medications in case one of them loses or forgets theirs and whatever it would require to care for them if they have a flare-up or reaction to anything we encounter. Before I forget, I did get the water purification tablets should that emergency arise, along with bottles for every member of the team. I've got the radiation badges, Geiger counter and radiation poisoning equipment. I know we're basically unreachable so I'm trying to be prepared for everything.

That's why I chose you Myra. Well that and you're so doggoned pretty. I can't help it. You're like my little sister and I have to pick a little and keep you on your toes. I'm sure you've gotten everything we could possibly need. You're top notch, that's why I was insistent you be the medic on this expedition. It's really happening Myra. We've waited a long time for everything to come into place and I'm so glad it has.

You've got this Tom, you have a great team assembled and we know the plan, the risks and the amazing outcomes when it's all finished. Take a breath now because you won't have time later.

Denver
Thanks for choosing me and letting me know so quickly. I'm nearly packed. I have a lot of gear. I hope that won't be a problem. It's almost all

survivalist stuff, I don't want anything to cut short our time there. We're going to need every body and every minute to pull this off. I know that if we manage to do it on the first try, there will still be trials and consistency tests to be done, so I want to be ready. I've read everything I can find on the location and it looks like we'll have everything we need to survive should all our supplies be lost or damaged. I'd kind of like to try out a few of the things, but I sure don't want anything going wrong that I'd need to. Again Professor Silvers, I do really appreciate this incredible opportunity and I'll work long and hard to help your dream come true. The participation credits alone will further my career so that one day I can be as published as you are and looked up to and revered as an accomplished humanitarian and scientist. I truly strive for greatness in our field of study and look forward to the day when I'm in your group of peers.

Margaret
Professor Silvers, you have no idea how excited I am to be included in your field trials and further study of time. Whether we can bend it, fold it, slice it, or create a portal, doesn't matter to me. Being a part of it all and learning so much from this experience is enough for me. I've dreamed of this day and cannot wait for this to begin. I'm thinking two weeks is a very long time to wait. I'll be going stir crazy. I've started packing my gear, drawings, notes, everything I've anticipated I'll need that could be of help to the project, plus the stuff on your list. I can never thank you enough for giving me this opportunity!

Alan
Wow, I'm so excited to hear from you. I've been

gathering things I think may be of benefit for us. My bags are packed and I'm ready to go. I started to bring maps, but figured I'd get lost anyway so I decided to leave that stuff up to Denver and Jody. They seem to know what direction is north after you've blindfolded them and spun them around fifteen times. They glance at the sky and take off in the right direction. I'm not that guy, but I am thankful I'm one of the guys you've chosen to assist you in the greatest experiment in the last thousand years. I've studied and studied your papers and I really think this will work. We have enough people monitoring everything and enough IQ to levitate a body if it worked that way. I am not going to be there to see if we can do it. I'm going to be there to watch it happen. You know you have every ounce of my brain and body available to get this job done. It's an adventure I want to go on. I'll take the first step through if you want me too. I'm ready for it.

George
Hey Doc. Good to hear from you. I've been going nuts getting stuff ready to go. I hoped beyond all hope I'd be on the team. I'm your quarterback, give me the ball and I'm running. I can't wait to step through whatever anomaly we create. Back in time, forward in time, folding into a different dimension, all that's cool with me. I can handle the 21st century's Flash Gordon persona. If I can help save the world once we open up this can of time, I'm your man. Time traveler extraordinaire! I've got the guts to help you achieve the glory. I know our small contribution credits will give us a major leg up in our careers and I do mean to go far. I want to create new powers to fuel our planet and fulfill the hunger our machines have for it. Can't wait to see you doc. Take care of yourself until I

can help do that for you. Dang! This is getting real exciting. I'm so pumped up, I can barely sit still and listen as you talk to me on the phone. Two weeks, they'll be long ones for sure.

Alison
Professor Silvers! I'm so happy you called, I was hoping beyond all hope that I would be chosen to participate in your experiment. I didn't want any trouble from anyone else who thought they should go instead of me, but I literally squealed when I saw your number on my phone. I've packed in hopeful anticipation and have only a couple things to add per your list I just received. I cannot tell you how honored I am just to be considered to work with you. I will do the very best job I can and will contribute as much as possible, physically and intellectually. I want to do this. I want to fix mistakes, travel through time, and relive precious moments in my life. All these things will be possible once you've perfected your formula for time shifting. I hope you've worked out the name for what it is we'll be accomplishing. I'll do everything I can to help coordinate everyone and help each person there do their very best work so this dream will become reality. Thanks again!

Steve
Oh my gosh! I'm so excited to hear from you. I knew you said it would be today, but I was beginning to wonder. I want you to know I won't let you down. I've gone over my lists four times and everything is ready to go. I even numbered my bags so I wouldn't misplace one of them. I truly consider it an honor sir to be on your team. I really mean it when I say I'll do everything I can in order to help make this a success. I've wanted a project

like this for years and I can hardly believe I have it. I'll work even harder than I usually do. You can count on me professor.

Ryan
Professor, it's good to hear from you. I've been running your numbers and I really cannot find anything out of place. I wouldn't be surprised if we nailed it on our first attempt. I know, before you interrupt me, there are more variables than the basic equation, but I still believe it will be all said and done way before our four months. If you want a volunteer to go through the portal, I'm your guy, just say the word and I'm yours. It would be the greatest day of my life!

Jody
Hello professor. I've been waiting on your call. I'm packed, and have gone over everything you gave me. I have weights on all the equipment and have expanded the equations for weight distribution once we start the human trials. Nothing is too heavy for one man to carry so moving and repositioning stuff will be a breeze. I can't wait to get started. This chance means the world to me professor and I won't forget it either. If you ever need me after this project even, I'm here for you. I want you to believe I'll give it my everything, as much as if it were my own project. Thanks again!

Well those calls went well. Every single student knew they were going to be on the team. They'd already started packing and gathering their stuff. That level of confidence was a good thing to have on a project like this one. The good professor was surely lifted up and excited even more after speaking with them all. He had a team that was willing to go above and beyond to make his dream come true; and they were only getting minor credit for the success. It didn't matter, they knew how great this was and they'd recalculated everything that he'd given them and were just as sure as he was that this was going to work. They would all be published in every science type journal in the world. They would be heroes in every magazine that hit the shelves in America. They'd be celebrities making the round of talk shows, explaining in language a five-year-old could understand; because when it came to science and energy, tachyon pulses and the like, the only thing most American's knew about it all came from watching Star Trek or Star Wars. They had no knowledge or understanding of what it took to open a window or portal in time. They'd seen H.G. Well's version of a time traveler, but they really didn't know how it worked and it certainly didn't work like in the movies. This was reality and it could be dangerous. Everyone on the team knew that and respected the powers they would be using to find that chink in time that they could pry into; to open up a whole new way of living. He had a few things he'd like to fix in time, himself; but that would require a lot of study to keep the repercussions down to a minimum. Every move we make affects everything else in motion in this time or any other time we might travel.

Chapter 3

The two weeks flew by. Tom went over every calculation three more times, triple checked his gear, bought more extra batteries and power packs. He was as ready to go as he could possibly be and he was as nervous as a groom on his wedding day. He'd worked on this baby for years and was now down to the final hours of labor before it would be birthed. It was scary and exciting at the same time. So much could go wrong, but so much more could go right!

He'd arrived at the pick-up location two hours early and had greeted everyone as they arrived. Exactly at six o'clock, the helicopters started landing. Crew jumped off and started putting their gear into big plastic crates. Each had a cable attached to it and would be lowered to the ground at the site. It was a mere twenty five minutes until they were lifting off. It was only twenty more minutes until they, along with their equipment, were being lowered at the test site. The army and NASA teams had taken over. The men dropped first and took control of every person and box that came after them. Once they were all unloaded and safe on the ground, the men were lifted back up to the helicopters. The crew chief radioed them to verify they had communications and to tell them they had exactly four months before extraction. There would be daily flyovers at six each morning to radio supply requests for the next day and drop off anything requested from the day before. If they missed the flyover, there would not be another one for twenty-four hours. They were officially a military team and would abide by military rules, lingo, chain of command, and responsibilities.

Tom gave Denver the go-ahead to take control of where everything would be set up, from the camp stove to everyone's sleeping quarters. It was a busy two hours, but with him in charge and everyone cooperating to the fullest, they'd gotten everything set in its designated location. Another four hours had all the tents up, equipment in place and lunch was cooking. After it was all laid out, each person took command of their quarters, the three women bunked in a large tent together, the guys split into two groups of three per tent, the professor had his own tent, there were two portable latrines set up, two portable outdoor showers, a supply tent, a medical tent, a communications tent and a strategy tent. They could have met outside; but if it rained, all the notes, plans, data and such would be destroyed in the rain, plus there was room for it, so they opted to bring the extra tent, tables and chairs. It would also make a nice mess hall at meal times. It was a top-notch military grade facility in the middle of nowhere.

Next thing was for them all to take a walk of the camp and close surrounding so they'd know their way around. They loaded up on the insect repellent and headed off behind George, he just seemed to be the natural leader in most everything; but he knew his strengths and weaknesses as well as when to let someone else lead. That's what real leaders excel in and he would make for a great president one day if he so chose. They trekked a one-mile perimeter from the camp. Denver marked trees strategically but not too obviously, so if one of them did become lost, they could find the tree and it would point towards the camp. It was an easy system Denver had for marking the trees. Exactly two feet up the tree, he would scratch the marker. It was less than an inch in size, but pointed left, right, up or down to show you the direction you needed to move in. If you saw the down, you were to take extreme caution as you were in a very visible spot and should get behind the tree and wait to check if you had company around you before you proceeded to move towards camp. It seemed a little melodramatic, but this was a big deal and there were governments, companies and mercenaries that would love to get their hands on this technology. It would change the power status of any country that possessed it and would also bring a huge price from anyone wanting to sell it to the highest bidder. It had to be kept "Top Secret" At the four compass points, he placed spare walkie-talkies in zip lock bags and buried them at the base of the marker trees in shallow holes, just in case someone needed help and theirs was out of power or had gotten dropped. Just another precaution from the expert in the group.

Everyone carried their walkie-talkies and checked them out. They worked together to climb over or under anything in their paths. They found the easiest access to their water supply, as well as some berries that were almost ripe. Jody did remind them all that there are bears and other wildlife for them to watch out for should they decide to go berry picking on their free time, the animals liked berries too.

It truly was a beautiful place, so untouched by man. The animals seemed to be so calm and only scattered when they got too close. The foliage was amazing. It wasn't like the rain forest's canopy, but these trees were thousands of years old and their circumference and height was a witness to that fact. The stream was so clean and cold. Except for the survivalists in the group, they'd never tasted water so pure. There were flowers still living here that had died out in most areas of the state. The beavers were busy as were the squirrels and birds, gathering in for the winter and reinforcing their nests. They all felt safe and happy here away from all the hustle and bustle of the cities and even small towns. Nature could truly be appreciated in this environment and they were taking it all in and enjoying every minute of it. They were pointing out different birds to one another and trying to identify them by their calls. They looked for tracks and "signs" of animals in the area. Along the stream, they found and identified the tracks of raccoons, deer, bear, squirrels, several birds, a coyote, and what they were pretty sure was a mountain lion. That track sent more shivers down spines than the bear tracks did. The clean fresh smell of pure nature was all around them. Nothing like the air purifiers or fresheners they had at home, but truly fresh air that awakened your senses, and the smell of the water was refreshing, not filled with chlorine and fluoride. It all just tingled the senses and rejuvenated the body. The more strenuous parts of the hike, just made them breathe it all in deeper and truly kept them from being tired. It was nature's healing for every part of the body and they were reveling in it.

By bedtime that evening, everyone had already unpacked their personal belongings and they'd had two briefings on the plans for the next day, the layout of the land and the duty roster. Everyone would take turns cooking, cleaning up, and gathering firewood and water, so the schedule was posted. The only way they could get out of one duty was to trade off for another. Denver had already volunteered to take water duty for all three women in exchange for cooking time. He wanted to eat well and didn't want them to have to carry heavy buckets of water up the hill. He had the muscles for it and they had the cooking skills he preferred over his own. Ryan also made that deal as he wanted the lifting to keep his strength and muscles bulging. The ladies loved his "guns" but he was clueless to his physical attributes. He barely noticed the women, but when he did, he was the supreme gentleman. His mama taught him well, he knew exactly how to treat a lady. There were a few more trades and everyone knew pretty much what they were doing every day. They realized that this could change to some degree on a daily basis as there could and would be things popping up that would necessitate a trade. They all seemed pretty flexible and no one had issues with doing their fair share of the work.

They'd made good time in setting up camp, doing their twelve mile hike for directional purposes, safety markers and equipment. When they got back, they fixed dinner and by the time they'd eaten it was dark. Everyone knew what was expected of them the next day. They were going to do their first experiment. They were all very excited about it, but their bodies were pretty tired from all the physical exertion they weren't used to; so they turned in early to get as much rest as they could in their new environment.

It would take a day or two to adjust to the sounds of night in the deep forest and not jump at every sound; but they reminded themselves of where they were and that they were not alone and well equipped to scare off any predators that came too close to camp. In the first two minutes after retiring, they identified the coyote's howl and the owl's hoot for sure; but there were many other sounds they didn't know and branches popping or creaking in the wind that stirred. Like a house, there were always sounds it made and you had to get used to what they were before you could get comfortable. Their new "house" was sure settling from the disturbance they'd made during move-in. Still they were tired enough it wasn't too many minutes before they were all sound asleep.

Chapter 4

Morning came with the sound of a helicopter overhead. It was their six a.m. wake up call, courtesy of the military. Tom was up already and on the walkie-talkie telling them everyone was alright and there were no needed supplies for tomorrow. Everyone else sprang into action getting dressed, having breakfast and gathering their stuff for the day.

Tom gave a quick speech about time travel being in their eminent future and thanked them all for helping.

On the walk the night before, they'd chosen the spot for the first experiment. A nice clearing was about a half mile away. It was pretty secluded but very open, like some settler a hundred years ago had cleared the land for building a homestead and then just left it. It should have grown up a lot, but it hadn't. Probably poor soil was the culprit. Never-the-less, it should be a perfect spot for trials.

They were starting with nuclear power. They would need a cross power grid, with four point location. So the energy would be fed into a center machine which should use that power to cause a time distortion. Once the distortion was caused, then there were other calculations to control it. They had directional beacons that could take the energy from the center machine and direct it towards a certain coordinate and basically slice open the time channel at that location. Time portal for laymen and Sci-Fi fans. There would be a base at that location that would surround whoever or whatever was standing or located on that platform. That person, animal, or piece of equipment would have a set of coordinates with a time date stamp so the energy could direct them to that specific date and time at that exact location and then the box would have coordinates to return them to that location. If it was a manned trip, they could change the coordinates once they arrived in order to return back home or travel to a new destination. They were doing the first experiment with a squirrel in a box attached to the device. It was set for fifteen minutes into the future. This would test the directional coordinates, a living organism and the launching/landing pad all during the first trial.

They had assembled everything at each point of the circle and set all the coordinates. They all took a deep breath and started the countdown. They chose two minutes so everything could have its own checkpoint before the final switch was thrown to start the whole process. Launch pad-check. Coordinates-check. Squirrel-check. Power source directional beacons-check. Center machine-check. 10...9...8...7...6...5...4...3...2...1 Launch!

They all were intently watching that squirrel in the box through their protective eyewear as the professor hit the button. There was a flash of light and beams of electricity converged on the center box, but when the directional beacon directed that power from the center box to the squirrel, the only thing that happened was the squirrel was cooked immediately, and to an extremely well done condition. Fortunately they had about forty duplicates of everything needed for the experiments as the box for coordinate settings was fried as well.

The platform and everything else was unharmed. They'd have to check to see if they needed to run a ground wire to the unit. It could be as simple as that; so they tested it without the control box, just a piece of wood and the ground. It worked like they anticipated it would, so they were back to re-testing with the squirrel in the box. No success.

They all had a pow-wow to discuss what they'd learned and what their thoughts were on what to try next. They came to the conclusion that the power was too great once it was focused through the center box by the directional beacon, so they recalculated a few scenarios and came up with a lower power manipulation. It was trying to work without a lab where you could just build whatever you wanted to at any time. In the field it was a little trickier and a little more tedious, but they managed because they had the IQ to use whatever means they had to make it work. This time the experiment was a partial success. There was no damage to the box or the squirrel, except for his nerves maybe. They were sure he got quite a hair-raising experience from the static energy if nothing else. His heart rate was good and they gave him some water and nuts. He ate good and calmed down. He was basically unharmed. He wanted out, but no more than he would have should no experiment have taken place. They just didn't like captivity; and who can blame them, no one does. Ok, one problem fixed, now why didn't it send him some-where. They checked and rechecked all the settings just to be sure that all was in order and it was. Next step then, they decided, was that the power wasn't the issue, it must be the kind of power they needed. A lower grade or higher grade of energy. Radiation had to be a factor, so tomorrow they'd try magnetic energy. It should be easy enough to create the same amount as the nuclear energy so the only change would be in how the power was produced. Tom still had the sneaky feeling that environment might make differences too. So they secured the things they could safely leave without fear of destruction and carried the rest back to the camp.

Once they were all together, they talked it over again and threw out anything they could think of that may have kept it from working, or anything they thought might correct the error in calculation they had. After they'd decided on their approach, they then gathered what they'd need for the next day, so they'd be ready for an early start. They were ready for dinner, and even though Alison suggested they have squirrel, they all unanimously answered "NO!" After much laughter, she started cooking spaghetti. It was a pretty quick meal to make and since everyone was hungry, she figured it was the best thing to go with that day. While it was cooking, she made salads for everyone and toasted some garlic bread and they all enjoyed it very much. Jody brewed coffee and tea for everyone.

They talked a while about the experiment, the squirrels and their thoughts about it all. Even a little small talk about each other. They wanted to get to know one another and this is how you did that. They all knew of each other, but some had never talked before meeting to come here. Jody expressed his sorrow over the squirrels and of course got the title of tree hugger handed to him. He informed them he was an environmentalist, but not opposed to eating meat or cutting down trees, he was just about protecting what should be.

Finally the yawns outweighed the conversation, so one by one they headed to their tents to get ready for bed. They'd worked out the shower situation and half would shower in the mornings and half would shower in the evenings, so it wouldn't take so long at any given time. Of course if they ran into any skunks, they were all entitled to showers. This general decision was agreed to by everyone immediately and once again, they were working well together. Tom was so happy with his group.

Myra called Tom aside to talk a minute. She felt he might be disappointed in the fact that things didn't go so well on their first day; but he was really doing fine. He didn't expect perfection on the first day. If he had, he'd have only brought one power supply, one box and one squirrel. He knew it would take time and adjustments and changes, but he also felt they'd be minor things and their goal would be met within their timeframe.

She gave him a little pep talk anyway and reminded him Edison failed 1000 times before he made the light bulb. The point was to never give up. As long as there is hope, there is perseverance. They had four months to get this. They'd already eliminated two problems in the first day. She thought that was pretty good and Tom did agree. She told him every day would get them closer and for him to have a good night. He hugged and thanked her and assured her he really was ok. He also told her she was forgetting he called her his little sister and he was supposed to be the one giving encouragement. Then he winked, hugged her again and said good-night.

Chapter 5

Every scientist had ideas of grandeur about different areas within the field of science, but Tom had gotten bit by the time traveling bug when he was a just a boy and read the many stories by Jules Verne. Verne had written about traveling around the world, under the sea and even to the center of the Earth. Tom wanted more than anything to be able to do those things. He dreamed of what creatures he'd find when he went under the sea and what adventures he could get into as he traveled around the world. He knew early on that he wanted to be a scientist and as he grew, he knew going to the center of the Earth was pure fantasy. Even if it could be done, the human body wouldn't be able to survive it. He knew these stories were just a man's hopes and dreams that he visualized in his mind and wrote on paper so others could join him in his quests for the impossible. Tom also knew that some things he'd read about could be done and some things might be done if the right person worked hard on the right problems and found the proper solutions to make them work.

He knew he wanted to be the first real time traveler, so he spent his life chasing his dream and finding kindred spirits to join him in his quest. If he succeeded, he'd not only be famous, but he'd be fulfilled. He would be able to use this power to help right wrongs and change the future. He envisioned himself as the champion of time and our history changer. He wanted the world to be a better place and some minor changes in the past would bring immense results into the present he was currently in and into the future for everyone.

As he aged, he became very aware that this technology, in the wrong hands, could be fatal to the entire world; so it had to be guarded by a secret band of scientists who knew and understood the risks of time travel and what good and bad could be done with it. He knew he wanted to be the leader of this group, but he also realized the governments of the world would want this power as well. He had to figure out a way of keeping it a secret if their mission succeeded. He'd need the cooperation of the team to help him with the corrections through time; as well as the secrecy of it all. The very first thing they did, that caused a major change in history as they knew it would be noticed by a few and that few would certainly be government people since the best of the best worked for the government. If one thing was noticed, they'd work diligently to discover who had done it. He and his team might have to go underground. Become the nameless and faceless bunch of wanderers who would be hunted for the rest of their lives, or until they were found out. He was taking a big chance with NASA involved, but he had to have their resources in order to make it happen. He'd set his resolve not to show too much emotion over any success. He'd downplay it as much as possible until he found out if he could really trust the entire team.

His calculations were not wrong, he knew the first experiment would fail. He had to make it a struggle till the end. If it happened too quickly, they'd have no time to prepare his demise and cover up the success of the experiment. No one, but this team could know and it would be better if none of them were really sure. It would need to look like an accident. An accident that couldn't be disputed. There had to be enough evidence, bones, dental appliances, and such to supply the evidence needed to put everyone's mind at rest that he was dead and they had failed to complete time travel. It would be just another failed government grant.

Tom did have a plan and a pretty good one to fix things in the world. He'd be making small, short trips through time to make the big change and then subsequently make many smaller changes in time after the effects of that change caused the future time from the change to be different. He had to do it before it could become too evident. He would be jumping very quickly from date to date at exact pinpoint positions to make more changes to avoid detection of himself and the fact that the past had been changed by those in his time that would be watching. It was extremely detailed and every date and location was in his journal. It too was hidden in the past and that would be his second destination. From there he would have everything he needed to fulfill his dream. The world would have another chance. It would have another chance to do better and not corrupt the planet and the people in it. He could eliminate most of the crime and sickness, death would be a different experience for most. He had technology to secure life in stasis until cures for diseases could be found and they would be found because millions of lost records would be restored through his travels. Once he returned, this current world would be like Heaven and the technology he'd bring back would be supreme knowledge to do all things. His only problem was to start it all, he needed the power supplies from NASA and a trusted assistant to put him in the right place while they pulled the trigger so to speak. Once the first jump had begun, his time machine would be self-sufficient and not need the initial boost from the experiment. His first jump would be one minute into the future to blow up all the camp, notes, and equipment used in his trials. There would be nothing left for them to look through or find that would give them enough information to believe anything other than the fact that he was dead. He would be blown to bits in front of them all and the experiment would be a disaster and supreme failure.

The only issues would be getting everything down to the second. Once they'd done the initial test and they knew it worked with the squirrel, then when they were all asleep, he and his assistant would sneak out and send him on his way. They'd all be awakened by the explosion, as soon as they all ran toward the clearing, he (in the future) would drop a piece of the tank into the camp and everything there would explode. He'd drop a few more pieces of the equipment in the area, causing explosions and all would be over for NASA and the team.

Today was truly the beginning of the rest of his life. He was so excited, he could barely act even a little upset about the first failures. Everything was going as planned and soon he'd be helping the entire world, securing the futures for them and their generations to come. He would not be famous, no one would know his name or what he'd done for them, but he would know and that's all that mattered. The unsung hero wasn't a bad title for a man who'd given his whole life with no thanks thus far.

He'd preliminarily decided it should be Steven and would try to talk to him a little bit alone in the next day or two to see what his feelings were on the matter. His whole plan would require assistance from someone as he wanted to make sure everyone was safe and that someone was there to explain what happened to everyone else, including the government.

Chapter 6

There it was promptly at six, our extremely loud helicopter alarm clock. Tom was on the radio telling them we were good for the day, but many more days like this and we'd need more pieces of equipment built. They should hold just a bit before the order was placed however; but everyone was fine and nothing was needed at the moment.

They all began moving, getting dressed, getting breakfast started, doing their morning chores and gathering the required equipment to head over to the clearing for the day's experiment(s). Breakfast was a little more substantial since they would skip lunch and just have a snack. Then after about ten hours of setting up and conducting the experiments, they'd call it quits for the day, return to camp, clean up, cook and have dinner.

It was Alison's turn to cook breakfast and she was a self-proclaimed biscuit guru. So it was gravy, biscuits, sausage, fruit, butter, coffee and milk. She had asked Denver to build her an iron skillet cooker. It was a log, stood on its end with about 5 cuts into the top to give it room to breathe, but not pop all the way open. You put lighter fluid inside the cracks and then lite it. It would burn from the inside of the log and since it was flat on top, the skillet sat right there the whole time. Because of the cast iron, it conducted heat just like an oven, so biscuits were super easy to have in the middle of the wilderness. She had a skillet full of sausage and had decided to add potatoes to the menu, last minute, so they were cooking in another skillet on the camp stove. As soon as the sausage was done, she'd make the gravy in that skillet and it should all be ready at the same time. It was forty-two minutes from beginning until time to eat and that wasn't bad when you're cooking from scratch for ten people. It was a hearty stick to your ribs kind of meal that would certainly hold them all till dinner time, with the boost of a granola bar or a half peanut butter sandwich snack. She'd prepared the sandwiches as breakfast was cooking and filled the back-pack cooler with water, fruit and the sandwiches. She decided at the last minute to put the leftover bacon on a couple biscuits in case someone wanted that for their snack.

When the party took off to the experiment site, Steve would always be the last in line so he could make sure everything was secured, off and no fires were left burning. He wanted no surprises and if a stray bear entered the camp, he didn't' want him finding any reasons to come back. If he couldn't get to the food and none was left on the ground, then more than likely he'd move on and not return.

He carried his share of stuff to the site, but brought up the rear to look for stuff that needed fixing, changed, or stowed away. He also kept a close watch behind as they walked as he knew all too well the danger they'd be facing if some spy or mercenary found out about their project and found their site. After all NASA was making regular helicopter flights to this same destination every day. He thought he might mention that to Tom so they could arrive from a different direction or base. Maybe even skip a day or two here and there. This was too critical to fall into the wrong hands.

Chapter 7

It was time for the second day of experiments, and they were all excited. They set everything up as they had the day before, except for their power source. Today it would be magnetic power. It would take a little time to get the electrostatic field generated. Magnets could hold their power for quite a long time, but it also took a little bit to generate the energy they'd need for this experiment and this magnet hadn't been charged. They'd done that on purpose so it wouldn't create any problems during transport. Creating a hole in time wasn't a job for the Energizer Bunny. They needed his whole family to get that going. While they were waiting for enough power to build to activate the magnets, they decided it was time to get to know each other a little better.

Tom, bowed out, saying he wanted to calculate and recalculate the formulas. He'd done that about a thousand times already, but they were scientists, so they knew they'd be doing the same thing if it were their experiments, and if he wasn't doing it, some of them would be.

Myra started, of course being a doctor was pretty much a given that just about the whole world knew what she did, so she told them the things she enjoyed. A quiet evening on the porch where there was no traffic, lightening bugs and/or stars was very much preferred. A gentle stirring of air to push the heat past you, making it oh so comfortable in that swing you were sitting in. She liked to read there with a big glass of sweet iced tea within reach and plenty of mosquito repellant on so she wasn't eaten alive. She also liked the beach, sunsets, sunrises, and flowers. Magnolias were her favorite, they smelled heavenly. She laughed. "I may have lots of brain power, but I sure like to put it on hold when I can and just relax and recharge. And if you'll notice all those things I mentioned are very calming, non-electrical, natural things that relax the mind and body."

Denver said he liked anything that moved, human, animal, creatures, vehicles, time and space. He didn't care what he was studying, but if he had two minutes on that porch with Myra, he'd have killed all the mosquitos, caught at least twenty five lightening bugs, swept away all the spider webs and squished the spiders. He might have time to gulp down a glass of tea, but the sunrise and sunsets took too long to happen and flowers, while fragrant and smelled so much like a woman or vice-versa, that was about all the use he had for them. He was all about moving and looking for ways to improve motion, either make it faster, more fuel efficient or trained to move fluidly. Relax? He did that with a knife in his hand, or a shovel. His only real hobby and it was a slow one, was whittling. His grandpa had taught him and he couldn't do it very often, it required too much sitting still. When he did, however, sit still that long, he carved some very intricate patterns in wood or bone. He liked animal scenes in particular, but he also did an amazing celestial one in an elephant tusk. It took him months to do as the tusk was over five feet long and he carved both sides. "Now that was almost too much relaxing." He laughed. Myra commented that while he was burning the candle at both ends now, age would compensate for much of that later. He'd learn that down time was much needed and could be thoroughly enjoyed as well as the fact that many ideas were generated in the stillness of doing nothing but contemplating the work you're doing or the work you'd like to be doing.

Several of them commented that it was nice to get to know a couple things about each other. It helped them appreciate their minds better when they seemed human in it all as well; not just driven to do experiments whether they would help people or just for the sake of doing them to see what would happen.

Margaret, as they'd learned already liked to mix things. She attributed that to her easy bake oven she had as a small child. She'd take the packets that came with it and change the ingredients to make something knew. Once it took her three days to get all the dough out of it because she'd left it to rise in the oven instead of on the counter. It filled the whole oven and spilled over the sides. She was definitely into quantum physics. That's why cooking was so important to her, she could mix different things and watch their reactions to the other ingredients or the heat from the oven or stove. She laughed when asked if she had similar results with the power of her new bomb. How many exploded ovens did she have before she perfected that formula? "There was a lot of testing, I'll say that much; oh and eyebrows grow back at a pretty good pace." They even heard Tom chuckle at that one. He may be calculating, but he was also paying attention. She said her favorite thing to do in the summer was wade barefoot in the creek behind her house. The water would be so cold and the rocks felt so smooth under her feet, it was like a spa treatment for her. It was very invigorating with the cold water, but still very relaxing as the stress just seemed to wash away down the stream. She admitted to being a tomboy growing up and still could hit a curve ball at the family reunion baseball game.

Alan didn't really want to talk about himself much but with some urging, he finally gave in. He admitted to getting lost if he had to make more than two turns to get somewhere. He'd even had to call home and tell his parents what street he was on so they could come get him or tell him how to get home. The worst time, and he was getting pretty upset about not being able to find his way home, he was two blocks down and one block over from his house. He didn't do much outdoorsy stuff at all. He did like watching sports and even playing a couple. Basketball was his favorite. He wasn't real tall, but he was real quick and would steal the ball more times than they could count. He won a couple awards in high school for high scoring and such, but his real passion was math. He'd play math games all day long, or until his mom kicked him out of the house to go get some exercise. When he was real little, he'd make pyramids out of his toys and conduct ratios and make them into bar graphs and pie charts. He never played with two toys that were not the same color or at least a shade of that color. There could be a hundred out at the same time, but they all had to be in the same color group. "Weird, I know." he smiled

George was the jock. If there was a game going on, he'd be playing it. He was on the football team, the basketball team and the soccer team in high school. He never missed any of the games and played in ninety percent of them too. His favorite game though was horseshoes. He played that with his dad, grandpa and older brother. They had quite the family rivalry going; but it was all in fun. Everyone had their own technique of how they held the shoe, which foot was in front when they released it and who pitched with an arc and who threw flat shoes. He was a flat shoe pitcher and was hard to beat too. For relaxation time, he played guitar, mostly oldies from like the fifties and sixties. Those songs had good rhythm and you could understand all the words. They were songs that said something, they didn't just have a beat. He also loved ballads, of course that's what made him popular with the ladies. Maybe he'd play them something at the campfire that night before bed. His other passion was power, anything with power, anything that used power, anything that could be changed to generate power was his mainstay. It was all about the power! He wouldn't even mind the power of the presidency one day if he could find the right woman to help him get there. He knew from recent history, that it was the women who got the men where they were. He wanted a strong one too, in another twenty years, maybe. Well maybe forty was too old for marriage, but he didn't really have too much time for women in his life right now; or not women that were around for more than a couple months anyway. They just took up too much of his time. When he went into overload and had to rest, he'd go in a dark room, pull the covers over his head and sleep. He would play soft music very low in the adjoining room. He might sleep for fifteen hours when he crashed, then he was good for another couple months or longer.

Alison loved to cook as evidenced by breakfast. She painted, wrote poetry and liked to go for long walks in the forest or park, wherever she could get to so that she could commune with nature. A nice babbling brook would do the trick for her. She was in love with nature, but not in the save the planet way. She just felt better among the bugs and leaves. She'd take her paint supplies or her journal and then decide when she got there what she felt like doing. It was peaceful and many times, she'd get a brilliant idea or two while she was there. She'd started two small businesses and was doing quite well with them both. She liked to sing, but was afraid to sing in front of people, maybe that's why she enjoyed the long walks in the woods. They made her promise to sing with George that night before they'd let her quit telling all her secrets. She was secretly hoping she didn't know anything he'd want to sing.

Steven was the anal one in the bunch. They'd all witnessed his checking something and rechecking it and sometimes checking it again. He was rather obsessed over stuff. He did admit that to unwind, he did yoga and listened to meditation music. He thought he had an out of body experience once, but realized he'd just cut off his oxygen and passed out. He had his head bent between his legs and his arms twisted into a pretzel pattern around his torso. He'd apparently been that way a while and lost consciousness. When the laughter died down, he continued to tell them he slept in a hammock at home to eliminate the pressure on his spine and lift his spirits and imagination up as he slept. He was an amateur magician, which goes against everything science upholds. He also believed that everyone really knew that there isn't real magic, but the sleight of hand and tricks to the eyes that make "magic" work and people think something just happened that couldn't really happen in reality; but he couldn't help but love it when someone smiled as he completed the trick, he was in heaven! The star of the show!

Now Ryan on the other hand was a numbers guy. He could see them in his mind and figure out patterns and related paths between a set of them. He needed to escape his mind more than most of them. So not to think, he'd relax using physical activity, but quite unlike George who was the ultimate jock, Ryan danced. He didn't do anything professionally, although he was good enough to, he would just crank up the music and dance for an hour. Then he'd be tired and his mind would be rested. Sometimes it took an hour of dancing every six to eight hours when he was really stressed, but it worked. It was just a hard method to do around people. Now the brainiac part had researched every dance known to man and he'd taught himself at least fifty different kinds of dance. He was slightly lacking in ballroom since you need a partner and partners distracted him from learning the dance moves, but he was working on those as well, just for social skills. He danced to some of George's favorite type music. Oldies and classic rock were his fav's. ABBA was especially easy to dance to. Oh and photography, but he was pretty technical with that. He liked all the right filters, lighting and effects so that wasn't as relaxing as dancing, but it was his hobby.

Which bring us to Jody. He was the guy you wanted working on your car or cleaning out your garage. He has muscle and didn't care to get dirty. He was a go-getter and they'd witnessed that first hand when unloading the boxes and setting up the camp. Jody's favorite hobby was working on machines, motors, cars, heavy equipment, whatever. If it ran and used oil or grease, he wanted to get his hands on it. He was the rare breed who was super intelligent, could work with his hands and not just his mind, and was sensitive, a ladies man, but not smug or hung up on himself. To have such a high IQ, he truly was grounded and humble if you would. He was a religious man and wanted to help others with his vast knowledge. He did volunteer work at the senior center where the folks would sign up for him to go to their houses and fix their lawn mowers, kitchen appliances, etc. He wanted to give back to those who'd already given their contributions, plus he learned so much from these folks. That was knowledge you couldn't get from a book. He attributed his well-rounded self to his mother. She'd taught him how to be self-sufficient so if he never married, he wouldn't be hungry or wear dirty clothes. He kept a very clean apartment and could handle himself in the kitchen as well. He wasn't worried about creating a future right now or settling down. He knew he had time for that and just felt it would work out by itself. One day he'd just meet the right girl somehow, somewhere and it would be love at first sight, or something very cliché he laughed. The other guys did too and the ladies sighed indicating that's every girls dream and some lady would be very lucky to find Jody in their lives.

Chapter 8

By the time they'd all talked about themselves and answered questions about their hobbies and interests, the machine was at full power and ready for the day's experiment. They all jumped in and arranged the equipment into the pattern they needed according to Professor Silvers' instructions and equations.

The magnetic field was at peak so Tom gave the countdown to activation. The magnets began to whirl inside their cylinder and after twenty seconds the final button was pushed to activate the sequence to open the curtain of time. There was a quick flash of light, a loud bang and the squirrel and his box were gone. Everyone shouted with pleasure and began clapping and high-fiving each other and for a wonderful minute and a half, they thought they'd done it. They thought that squirrel would be reappearing in another thirty seconds. There was more excitement in that short amount of time than all the people gathered in Time Square on New Year's Eve when the ball finally hit the bottom. Much to their chagrin, though, he appeared in the next two seconds. As Ryan turned around to hug Steven, he saw it. He saw the squirrel, not where it was supposed to be, not in the future or the past, but stuck firmly to the magnet, inside his metal box. What an immediate drop in excitement. He hadn't been shoved through time into the future. He'd been attracted to the magnet, so quickly no one even saw it move. Once the light was gone, so was the squirrel. They were all looking in the wrong direction to see it. It had been sucked past them so fast, none of them were able to see it go by. Everyone was stunned and stood looking from one to the other in the group, when all of a sudden George burst into song. "The day the squirrel went berserk, in the First Self-Righteous Church, in that sleepy little town of Pascagoula." At that, the whole group burst out laughing. It was the most unexpected thing that could have happened and there was nothing else to do but laugh. George explained it was one of his favorite Ray Stevens' songs and just seemed appropriate for the moment. They were all momentarily disappointed, but realized their mistake. They had not created magnetic energy, but instead a giant magnet. It's a wonder everything metal wasn't sucked up in one huge ball on the end of the magnet.

Tom laughed and said he supposed they might need a couple adjustments and how in the world did Steven not catch that possibility. Steven smiled a very sheepish smile and just picked up a wrench and said "We've got adjustments to make, somebody get that squirrel off our magnet so we can generate magnetic energy. I think we're ready now that the show's over. Well that is if everyone is through laughing." To which they all laughed again and then got started. Although they had some work to do, everyone was in a great mood. The failed attempt had been so unbelievable, that it left them all with high spirits. It would be the most memorable failed experiment in history. As soon as they achieved their goal and released reports of how it all happened, the whole world would be laughing about the magnetized squirrel. Alison retrieved the squirrel and put him and his box back on his pedestal awaiting another attempt at time travel. They were truly surprised the squirrel didn't have a heart attack when it all happened, but he didn't seem any more hyper than they usually were, so it seemed he was ready to get on with the show as well.

It took a couple hours to get everything re-calibrated, but they finally were confident everything was correct and they could start the countdown again. This time there was a flash of light, a lot of noise from the magnet, everything metal was trying to attach itself to the big magnet, but nothing happened to the squirrel. He was still sitting right there in his box when all the commotion was over. Another fail—not as funny as the first, but they were still light-hearted over it all. Tom said he didn't want to be Edison, but it looked like he was well underway to obtaining the honorary title.

They spent the rest of the day checking every calculation and made six more attempts, but it wasn't going to work. Every single one failed, so they decided to scrap the magnetic power and move on to laser tomorrow. They secured the equipment that was to be left at the launch site and carried the rest back to the camp. They were not sending anything back in case something came up and they needed something to use in conjunction with or to substitute for another option. They also didn't want NASA to know they'd failed with each power source, so keeping the equipment would keep everyone in the dark.

Tom suggested after dinner they go through with the sing-along to George's guitar music. Maybe even have teams and make a game of it to help everyone relax from all the stress and just enjoy their time together, getting to know each other more while being silly and letting their brains rest from all the concentration and frustration of the past two days. Might even cheer the squirrels up, he laughed.

Jody and Steven did dinner that night, they cooked cowboy style. They made baked beans, fried potatoes, cornbread (fried), and pork chops on the grill. It was really good and Alison surprised everyone with the ingredients to make s'mores. Since they were having campfire fun, she told them. They were the perfect ending to a great meal. Those guys could cook! She'd never had a grilled pork chop that was so tender. Kudos gentlemen from the whole team!

Chapter 9

There was NASA, right on time, with their wake up call. This strict schedule really suited all these geniuses so they didn't complain, they just got busy doing their things so they'd be ready to travel in time, hopefully before that day ended. So far that had been the hope all three mornings. None of them were discouraged yet, there were several more options they had to try before they became discouraged. There was still plenty of time to make it work and work out any kinks as well. They were mostly still in the awe stage of it all. Out of all the people in the world, they were the chosen to pull this off. What an honor given them and they appreciated it more than the professor really knew.

Now Margaret was all about mixing ingredients, thus the bomb making for the military. She created breakfast burritos, omelets and toast. They were hearty as well, with all the vegetables and meat inside. Plenty of protein with little carbs. Quite unlike the gravy and biscuits, loaded with carbs. No one complained though, as it was excellent food. Two of the guys were going to cook meals, but they were more dinner cooks, so everyone was looking forward to see how they compared to the women. The guys who traded cooking for more manual labor was truly thankful for the good cooks they had. They'd also had a good supply person who'd ordered enough stuff and the right stuff to make everything turn out just right.

It was just their third day, but they were all getting along and no problems had occurred as of yet and they really thought it would stay that way. Tom had picked a good team with all the right qualities.

They had three visitors on their way to the clearing...a whole deer family. Usually you never saw the buck with the doe especially if she had any little ones, but he stood proud and seemed to tell them this was his home and they needed to go around. They all agreed and did just that. It's the first wildlife that had ventured near them and they were hoping none bigger came by. Bears were so destructive when they caught the scent of food, they'd dig for days, pull stuff down or up, it didn't matter they didn't give up, so everyone was hoping none would make an appearance while they were there.

There were no other incidents on the way and it didn't take them but a couple minutes longer to get there via the longer route around the deer.

They began setting up the experiment, all the components were distributed, the poor squirrel from yesterday was given the day off, he'd be back tomorrow though, and the power source was the only thing left to go. They were using laser power. It was a tricky one because it had to be focused exactly or it would cut through whatever it was aimed at. There were special mirrors used to direct it and it worked well when set up properly. They didn't want to slice a squirrel or any trees either. It was Steven's turn to double and triple check before the laser was turned on, just to be sure.

They were ready for the laser test and everyone was holding their breath for many reasons and the greatest was that the beam was directed properly so as not to slice away anything living or important to the mission like a mountaintop. Now that would be noticeable from a few directions.

Nothing. Another failure. They tried two more times before lunch. They chatted through lunch about what adjustments could be made and none was found. They decided to try three more times after lunch with different power setting, but none of that worked either, so they decided laser was just not the right power source.

Now it seemed like they were speeding through their options, but getting rid of the unnecessary stuff very quickly kept the main playing field uncluttered. Tom wasn't worried, he'd worked on this nearly his whole life and had found great minds to help him bring it all to fruition. They were young minds, but none-the-less great!

He was going to talk to the kids about weather, atmosphere and local conditions to see what their take might be on that. It would be a good subject to discuss over dinner. He still felt those things would make a difference. He even had thoughts about atmosphere being like mood lighting or a romantic setting that could enhance or hide the effects of the power. Much like a woman could manipulate a meeting into a romantic situation if she so desired. He decided his "woman" of time and space may just need a little stroking to get in the mood to play.

It was George and Myra's turn for cooking and they decided to fix grilled chicken with rice pilaf, steamed broccoli with lemon butter sauce and fried apple pies for dessert. Sounded pretty fancy to

George for the woods, but he said he could handle the chicken and fried pies if Myra did the fancier stuff. Although she assured him it was really easy, he kept his part. She helped peal the apples for the pies while her vegetables cooked and after George had made the dough, she filled them with the mixture of apples, cinnamon, nutmeg, flour and sugar, he folded them over and dropped them in the hot oil to cook. It truly was a delicious meal. They got down to business while eating it though, to discuss the atmosphere and it's affect on the experiment. They decided the weather had little effect on it, but did believe that a tachyon pulse might be the boost needed for the power to be at full effect when it was released into the converter and directional beacon.

They each took pen and paper to devise their own calculations and theory on how to use the tachyon in the experiment. He gave them twenty minutes and then they would compare notes. At the end of twenty minutes they began to explain their notes and compare what they'd come up with. Surprisingly enough, or maybe not surprising at all, they were all pretty much on the same thought wave. They suggested one second pulses of the tachyon beginning two seconds before the power of the plutonium was released. And yes every single one of them suggested plutonium. It seemed they all felt it was the most stable and versatile means of power there was. It had seemed safe for people in the past with other experiments and was not too dangerous to use and transport. Scientists were making great strides in reducing the amount needed, the container size to hold it and the total function of it for commercial use. Tom was pretty optimistic for tomorrow's experiment.

Chapter 10

It was day four and Tom felt this was going to be the day. He woke up extra early showered, dressed and had breakfast cooking. He wasn't in the cooking rotation but he was too excited to sleep, and was overly chipper. He just felt it was going to be a great day. He had coffee ready and the bacon was almost done when the helicopter radioed. He instructed them everything was good, nothing needed and as everyone started filing out of their tents for breakfast, he was finishing the first skillet of scrambled eggs and had begun filling a plate full of toast. The couple people who didn't like scrambled, gave him their orders and he began cooking a half dozen over easy eggs for them. Everyone was giving him a hard time about being so excited. They knew that was what was up as they could feel it emanating from him. Ryan poured orange juice for those preferring that over the coffee and they were all ready to eat.

Another thirty minutes and they were off to the clearing, loaded with squirrels, plutonium, and the tachyon pulse emitter. Everyone was jolly and laughing, pointing out wildlife they'd startled with their laughter and then laughing again. It was time to disrupt time, and they were ready for it.

It only took about fifteen minutes to set up all the equipment and double check the plutonium container and ensure it was positioned correctly. Tom had given some last minute safety instructions should the Geiger counter start registering anything dangerous and they were in countdown mode. One minute countdown to test time. Everyone got behind the lead barrier for extra protection from any undue radiation emissions and Tom finished the countdown. At one, he engaged the system and everyone watched. The power moved through the air towards the squirrel in the box and then the tachyon pulse was triggered. It was active and pulsing at one pulse per three seconds. It was a mere twenty seconds before a heavy fog moved over everyone and a thick gooey substance covered them all. It was like puss oozing from an infected boil, thick, yellow and cold. As it rolled past them and approached the squirrel where all the power was directed, there was a bright light, like sunlight peeking in from the tiny gap in the curtain. When that light disappeared the squirrel was gone. They all cheered and jumped up and down. The fog was gone and so was the thick gooey substance. It didn't linger and left no residue on their skin or clothes. There were no effects from it any more than there was the heavy fog, but it was very weird when it happened. Alison said she felt like she was going to smother when it covered her face, but when she reached up to wipe it away, there was nothing to wipe. It had just been a sensation of the time distortion.

When the squirrel reappeared, they all exploded in cheers. They were hugging and congratulating Tom on their success. Myra headed over to check out the squirrel. There seemed to be nothing strange about him. He seemed very healthy and unharmed. She hurried back to the table to get the Geiger counter and test his level of radiation. It was well within normal and allowable readings. The counter wasn't even registering anything at that moment and hadn't registered any radiation during the test. She just wanted to be sure the squirrel didn't absorb any during the test. She certainly recommended they attach a radiation badge somewhere on the box to monitor during the next trial. Tom pulled the sensors from the cage and plugged them into his computer to check what he could about where the squirrel had gone. The temperature monitor was normal, same as the temp where they were. The vitals from the squirrel didn't change, no accelerated heart rate, breathing problems, his oxygen level remained the same. From all the data retrieved, there was no change at all. Now to send a camera with the squirrel and have his return be a half hour later versus a couple minutes. They had to know more before a manned trial could be done. He was attaching two cameras, a GPS to determine location, a water container to catch any moisture in the air, an oxygen monitor and an electronic clock to see if there was any difference in time. It would be good to know that when he left and when he returned he was in sync with the time and place he left. He also changed the coordinates on the return GPS location to six feet away. It was flat and solid so the squirrel would have a nice landing spot. He wanted to test the location coordinates so he'd know if he could transport precisely from location to location versus leaving and returning from the same spot. One of the cameras would have a forward view to see what was ahead while the other camera was set to record the readouts on the monitors they included. This would give them a double check on conditions should a monitor fail in transport, they would have the recordings of what actually went on during the test. He also increased the size of the container the squirrel was traveling in and would continue to do so as they increased the experiments until it was big enough for a man to fit inside. They had to prepare the way for human trials and this was a good beginning. They couldn't be careful enough due to human testing being the next step.

They got everything hooked up and all the added features as well. Tom gave the little guy a nut and went back to activate the machine again.

First the plutonium power was focused and then the tachyon pulse activated. Presto change-o, no squirrel. Then the hard part came, the wait. While they were waiting for the half hour to end, Tom decided he needed to talk to them about not revealing their success yet to the military. He was concerned they'd come in and forcibly take over the project. They all agreed that they'd go on as before and Alan even suggested they request a half dozen more squirrels so they wouldn't know they weren't having failed tests.

Well the time was almost up so they all got ready to spring into action when the squirrel reappeared. Exactly at the precise time they'd set the machine, the box with the squirrel reappeared. More cries of glee and then everyone was scurrying to do all the checks and download the data. They each took a monitor and downloaded it to a computer and then all the data was dumped into the mainframe. This was faster than having to wait for each one to download to the main database, as the downloading was the time-consuming part. Myra took care of the squirrel again and again no issues at all. He'd eaten his nut and even had a bowel movement. She was thrilled with that because it showed her there was no disruption in the body's functions during time travel. Every single test came back normal. He was in the exact place they programmed him to be he was just ahead in time when he reappeared. Had they brought him back the same second or minute, he'd just be six feet away in the blink of an eye. The forward camera confirmed this as they'd started recording before he left and that view never wavered until he returned and then it recorded straight ahead from his new location. The move for return entry into their time was successful, so moving around during time travel wasn't an issue. The cameras showed everything the same as the monitor readings they downloaded. Tom had them place a clock on a stump along with a camera and start recording. They marked the date, time and GPS coordinates so they'd have reference for the squirrel's trip back in time. The stump was in front of where the squirrel would be and it was recording facing the squirrel. At the marked time, they all got behind the camera and held up a banner saying welcome Mr. Squirrel so the squirrel's camera would record them in the past and they'd know it was exact.

Tom decided they'd do a one hour and an overnight test. The squirrel would be leaving as they went back to the camp for the night and returning once they'd returned to the clearing in the morning after breakfast.

The one hour test was perfect as well and they decided for the overnight test, they wanted five cameras total, one pointing in each direction and one pointing at the instruments. This would give them a better view of what was happening there. Did the fog and thick ooze appear when he was returning, or just on exiting as it had every time they sent him on his journey? It might also tell them what the fog and puss, for a better word at the moment, was. It seemed harmless, but it would be good to test it as well, if they could. As of yet they hadn't figured out a way to test it as it was like it had never happened. They could feel it on their skin and see it in the air, but when they went to wipe it from their skin, it was like it had never existed.

Chapter 11

Morning came and everyone was up early. It would do them no good to hurry, as Mr. Squirrel was scheduled for a specific time and would not make an appearance until that exact time. They all wanted to talk about it, so they took their time fixing breakfast and then enjoyed it at a most leisurely pace as they discussed the events. Tom reminded them the flyover would be in a few minutes and suggested most of them be in their tents so nothing looked out of the ordinary. They agreed and scurried to their places. Once the helicopter left, they returned to their places to finish talking before they started cleaning up and doing their chores.

Myra suggested they take some energy readings to see if the squirrel's energy was still in the location even when he was not in the location at that time, but in the future. They thought that was a good idea. If it was, they'd need to find a way to detect it should time travel become popular. If the traveler could be detected, he or she may be able to be apprehended or joined to help or stop them with whatever they were doing. They also may want to develop a cloaking device to avoid being detected as they moved through time if it turned out they could be detected.

They'd all watched every second of it happen every time, but it still seemed like a dream or a Sci-Fi movie playing out in front of them, yet they were the stars. Oh and Mr. Squirrel, of course, was the main supporting character. Ryan's analogy gave them all a big laugh, but it was true, it still seemed impossible to travel in time.

They were in the clearing a good half hour before the squirrel was to return so they took some energy readings. Another thought was to see if something or someone was in the spot where the squirrel was to return, would it alter course or just appear on top of whatever was there. They all agreed they felt it would not alter course as the coordinate couldn't be changed without another jump or trip happening; but they wanted to test to be sure. They gathered three big pieces of logs and stood them up side by side. This would give the box a level surface, and if it landed on top, would also tell them the descent back into the present would be a vertical drop. They suspected it would be, but always good to know. The box had not seemed to land hard in the first experiments, so it seemed there was a braking system, or at least a gentle return through the rift.

They were just so excited about it all, they could hardly contain themselves. "Ok, everyone, take your places." Tom exclaimed. They had ten seconds left and all the analyses would start again. They should have a lot of data this time since the trip was almost twelve hours long. They were all going to watch the camera recordings together and mark times for anything different on the video that could be looked for in person as they lived it that night. Tom also wanted to make sure nothing bad happened, like a bear coming through the clearing, they'd need to take protection; otherwise, if there were no events, so to speak, then they should be safe in the clearing instead of at the camp. The best part was, they were all going to take turns watching the video that night at the clearing to see everything on the recordings happen throughout the night and morning. If it was true time travel, every leaf that shook on the video would be shaking as they experienced it that night. Denver suggested they all have a nap before dinner, then they all stay in the clearing and watch all night or most of the night. They could go back to camp early in the morning for breakfast and their flyover and then come back to finish watching as the squirrel transported back to their time. It was just too interesting to miss any of it. They all agreed, so that was settled, a late night sleepover at squirrel's place. They were all so happy that things were beginning to happen, any little thing would set them to laughing and letting their emotions run freely. Jody said "This is better than getting to restore a '57 Chevy and those are way too cool!" They each had their own ideas of what it was cooler than, but that was ok, they were all unique people so they would have different ideas of happiness, but one thing for sure, they were at the pinnacle of success at the moment.

They were all thinking about the military and keeping their little secret, when Steven spoke up and made all their thoughts clear. "I just want to say that I believe what we have here is bigger than all of us and I'm afraid if we share it, we'll open a can of worms that will be strung out through all of history, not to mention our futures. I think we should finish our four months and do all the experiments we can do to perfect time travel and then deny everything to NASA and whomever else in the government. I'm sure there will be a time when someone else discovers the formula for it, but till then I think we should be the keepers of time. I think the professor can use us as needed to help conduct time travel projects to make small changes in the past that will have great impacts on our current situation and on our futures, but they'll have to be small so as not to draw attention to what's going on. I know we'll all be watched for quite a few years and probably interrogated individually. They'll tell each of us that the others confessed to finding the right combination to open portals into different times and maybe even dimensions, but I think we all stick with the squirrel was fried every time. We can tell the story of the magnetic trial when we thought it worked, but didn't. I just think the world will be safer if we don't disclose what we have. I'd also like to propose we all have a copy of the results on a USB drive, but only if each of us is confident we can secure it in some unknown location that should our lives be turned upside down and searched, they won't find the data. We've developed a bond already and I think we can all agree that this is the best plan of action. It's the best for now, for us, for our country and the world. What say ye all?"

They all agreed and Tom expressed how impressed he was with Steven for speaking up and the rest for agreeing to forgo the fame and glory for the good of mankind. He said he'd already decided he was going to ask them to do this, but was waiting for the right time and feared one or more of them may not agree. It pleased him so much that they were scientists with integrity. He also asked them all to think about what changes should be made in the past that would be subtle and make a great impact on mankind's welfare. They could be researching those things and weighing everyone's thoughts and taking input on how exactly to accomplish each task while they were still here together working on perfecting time travel and ensuring it's safety for him and anyone in the future using it as well as working to hide everything they needed to hide from the military. They'd have to find a place to put the data they'd need and secure it because they sure couldn't have it in their possession when they were retrieved as he believed that everything including their persons would be searched for evidence that they had indeed succeeded in their tasks.

Jody said he could build two of the machines they'd need to transport the professor, with a little help from Denver and George. They could put the extra one in the past or future whatever they decided and use the other to go back and forth. No they'd need to put it somewhere secure in the future so that he wouldn't have to build anything else to get to it later. They could take most of the plutonium, a tachyon emitter, cameras, monitors and whatever else they thought they'd need and put it all together in the future. They would store their USB drives in each of their futures as well so no matter what they tore apart, they wouldn't find because it wouldn't be there for a couple years down the road. They could have a small explosion that "destroyed" several pieces of equipment. Alan said he could rig that and gather enough odds and ends up to be scorched so that real equipment could be stored with the other stuff in the future.

Myra said she wanted a medical kit on that machine because they didn't know what they'd run into during travel and she wanted Tom or whoever else was doing the experiments to be safe. She said she'd tear up boxes and make it look like a bear had gotten into the supplies and destroyed most of the stuff she was going to take for the mission's medical kit.

They couldn't think of anything else they'd need at the moment to get the equipment they needed and fabricate a disaster that destroyed it all. Now, it should probably be a laser accident as it would be the most likely and the easiest to replicate a fake explosion with.

It was amazing that this group of students knew how to save the world when all the leaders of all the countries all over the world had no clue how to do it. These kids wanted the fame and glory. They wanted to show the world what amazing stuff we did here in the mountains of West Virginia, but more than all that, they wanted to do the right thing. It wasn't their IQ's that caused this; it was their great humanitarian hearts that made them ready to abandon the glory for the better good. There would be other experiments and discoveries, but there wasn't another planet or human life to be found anywhere but here on good ol' planet Earth.

Alison was in charge of copying all the data to a central place, separated into distinct files so it could be easily copied to the personal drives they'd all have. They all had jobs to do along with their continued experiments in time travel. They'd have to have everything done and erased off the main computer days before the final deadline just in case they had a surprise visit from someone at headquarters, so that meant they needed to concentrate on all this stuff that needed sent into the future as quickly as possible.

Margaret reminded them all that they had to have

more footage to show for four months of experiments than what they already had, so they had to actually do some experiments that they knew would fail and video them and document them to show they'd actually failed and they'd done the work required of them for four months. She said she'd work on video footage for that and then they'd have to film a few squirrels getting blown up and power configurations that were used in each one. She had to turn off the date/time stamp on all the cameras being used for that filming so they wouldn't know things were being spliced. She also wanted to be technical in that she wouldn't show any people in them, so as not to get clothes mixed up in any scenes.

They had a plan and everyone was on board with it. They had, however, created double the work for themselves, but they didn't care, it was worth it and when the time was right, they could discover time travel then. No one had to know they'd done it here on this project or at this time and date. It didn't matter how much work they had to do, their planet was worth saving and they were the team to do it!

For now, however, they had video to watch and then nap, dinner and video all night in real time with video from the future playing along with it. It wasn't even going to be boring, because it was a true breakthrough in particle manipulation, time distortion and the beginning of a better world for all mankind. How amazing to be a part of all that!

Chapter 12

They watched the video and there was nothing out of the ordinary, no dangers to worry about and nothing much going on. It would be pointless to watch if it wasn't what it was. They would be watching what was happening around them at that exact minute, but had been recorded a day ago. It was hard to wrap your mind around, but they had to experience it. No one on Earth had done this before. Or if they had, they hadn't told anyone of it. Maybe there were other time travelers out there living the same secret as they were. Maybe they were not the first ones, but tonight they were! Tonight they were victorious over time. Tonight they were the champions of the greatest discovery of all time. They hadn't personally done it yet, but each would have their turn once they were ready for human testing. Each one would hide their own USB drive so no one else would know where it was. They had to protect this secret and had vowed to do so at all costs. They were all thinking about where they would hide theirs, and what date, time and GPS location they'd have to travel to in order to do it. They each were thinking about all the people they'd love to tell, but couldn't. There could be no conversations about any of it except with one another and that had to be in person or with coded messages in small spurts. Alan had particularly been thinking about that and he'd devised a few code words for them to use, just in case they were being recorded or watched. He decided they could have that conversation as they re-watched the video in real time tonight, right now they all needed a nap to get them through the night.

Once everyone was up and ready to fix and eat dinner, they got busy with their chores and the cooking. They secured the tents and gathered their camp chairs and sleeping bags for the night under the stars, watching the present from the future. They were about to have dinner, but gathered snacks and drinks to take along. Alison, the girl with the surprise s'mores supplies for the campfire, was full of surprises again. They did plan on a small campfire, so she had a kettle, oil, popcorn, butter, and bowls in her stuff for a late-night popcorn with the movie surprise. It had only been four days, but this team was meant to be. They were comfortable with each other and understood not only the technical stuff they discussed; but were down to earth and knew enough about sports, leisure activities and individuality to appreciate each other and understand the feelings and emotions they each experienced. They were getting to know each other a little more and were securing a bond that would last the rest of their lives.

Tom said this dinner was a celebration for them all, so he grilled the steaks while others jumped in to prepare the side dishes. It was a simple steak and vegetable dinner, but it was a splurge for them and it included a nice bottle of champagne. Tom told them to remind him to break the bottle and put the pieces in their trash, so no one would think they had been celebrating any spectacular results they may have achieved, but they all knew they were.

Once dinner was over and things cleaned up and final stuff secured, they were off to the clearing. They laid out their chairs in movie theatre style in front of the laptop where they would watch the video. Their sleeping bags handy and light jackets should the night grow cold.

Alan told them of his code words for the future and advised them to refine any of them or add to, but they needed to be fairly common words that wouldn't be spotted easily.

"Hold on, I have to go to the bathroom." would mean we need to get together so we can talk.
"I did great on that paper I told you about." would mean, I've had someone questioning me again about the experiments.
"I'm thinking about a vacation." would mean, I'm getting stressed out and will probably disappear for a couple days or so, don't worry. (they all knew that was probably going to happen as the pressure they were about to endure would be great, but they had a solid story and it was true, so sticking to it shouldn't be hard.)
"I still think about those old songs we sang at the campfire." would mean their USB card was in jeopardy. They were being stored in the future and if a tornado ripped apart the house it was stored in, or if someone bought the property, then it would need moved so it wouldn't be discovered during construction or whatever happened to put it in danger of being found.
"I have a severe headache." Would mean not to trust someone they were aware of.

They all agreed these should cover the basics because if it were anything worse, the bathroom thing would work so they could get together and discuss it further, whatever it was.

They also agreed that they should remain in contact, just daily chit chat or every couple days, first of all because they really did want to keep in touch and secondly because a sudden phone call when they hadn't talked for months would be a tell-tale sign something was going on.

It was like a spy movie where everything was code. A real life cloak and dagger game, and they were all primary players.

"Now it's time for the video." Tom told them. They had a two minute countdown to the beginning. Once the movie started, everyone was in awe watching a leaf move on the screen at the same time it was moving in front of them, or a tree sway ever so gently in the light breeze, or the hoot owl sounding off in unison with himself. A twig snapping as a deer moved about or the chatter of a raccoon; everything was exactly the same and at exactly the same time. If they didn't know better, they would think the camera was on now recording what was happening at that moment instead of playing back what was recorded the day before. Anyone walking up and seeing it all would have no clue it was recorded the day before from the future. The only give-away at all, was their comments, laughter and noises they made as they changed positions or reached for a drink. It truly was incredible knowing what they knew and still experiencing it for real.

When they were half way through the video, Alison started popping popcorn. She figured they'd need it to help them stay awake and her tummy did just rumble. They all were surprised and welcomed the hot buttery popcorn. She gave them each a couple handfuls from the first batch and continued to distribute small amounts from the next two

batches until everyone had a good serving.
Tom was a super genius in their eyes and they were so fortunate to have been selected to assist him. It was an honor they'd cherish their entire lives. Unfortunately it was an honor they'd probably have to keep secret their entire lives as well. Who knew what the future held for them, but they were hoping they could help make it a better future for all.

When the squirrel was about to come back to this time, they watched very carefully for the fog and thick ooze and sure enough it was the same as when he'd left every time. They weren't sure what caused it other than like skin, there was leakage of skin cells or "puss" sometimes blood but always some sort of liquid when the skin was cut. Apparently there were time cells lost when time was sliced into for travel. It was the only explanation they could come up with. Something caused it and it had to be time cells or atmosphere, something. If they knew where to start or what to look for, they'd investigate it. Maybe see if it could be detected somehow. They were sure it could be detected, they just didn't know what to detect so they didn't know how to build a detector for it.

When the video stopped, they all just sat there quietly, not having words to express what they were feeling. Denver was the first to speak. "Alright pioneers, we've got to get back to the camp, crawl in our tents and hide the evidence from tonight. I'm going to get rid of the campfire wood, ashes and burnt grass so I'll be a little behind you all. Hurry though, we don't want to get caught." At that they all moved quickly, picked up their things and headed off to camp.

They arrived about five minutes before their flyover, so timing couldn't have been better. Denver heard it coming so he ducked into the latrine, just in case they could glimpse him from the chopper. Once they were gone, he put his stuff away and proceeded to shower and do his chores for the day.

They should have been tired from staying up all night, but they were full of energy and ready to do more tests so they could have an opportunity soon to do it themselves. They would certainly have a better appreciation for traveling through time than that squirrel did.

Tom was going to take it easy on them today so they could catch up on their rest, but then with all the secret stuff they had to do, they'd need to get busy again making it all happen. They also needed a place to hide it all until it could be transported into the future. They never knew when or if NASA would decide to drop in (literally) for an inspection. They wouldn't call it that, but that's what they'd be doing. His biggest fear was that they'd send someone in via the hiking trail and they wouldn't know they were coming until it was too late. That was another reason they needed to have a hiding spot that was convenient, but far enough away so as not to be readily seen before they could store it in the future.

He thought he might secure a storage building in the future and pay up front for it for five years. This would give him plenty of time for the government to leave him alone and a place to put all the equipment. He could take some on every trip he made until it was all built and secured safely in the

future. Once the human tests began, they could all make their trips to hide their USB cards.
They could also do tests into the past to see how it affected them and anyone else, in their real time.

He didn't want to jump in and start making a lot of changes until he was sure of outcomes. He also was contemplating some strategic investments that would provide him the resources to fund this project himself so NASA wouldn't be involved at all. That should help take them out of the picture so they wouldn't be investigating him and his team or trying to get their hands on his work, to use for their own agenda.

Really there were a million things he could do to make life easier on himself and a lot of other people, but the moral question was should he? Was it right to use time travel for personal gain? Should it only be used when the end results would affect a certain number of people? Maybe a million, but why should a thousand suffer when the cause could be fixed? If they went back with the cure to small pox, would our world be so overrun with people that it couldn't contain or replenish itself to take care of them. Maybe plagues were God or nature's way of eliminating the weak so the strong could survive. Should population be controlled? It could be with laws; laws that could be enacted a couple hundred years ago. But would that eliminate the great minds that have helped society? Would this team be eliminated because people were limited on how many children they could have? It really presented a lot of thinking and decision making before they changed anything. There could be repercussions they'd not thought of in every action they took, because every action taken in the past put them where they were today; and today was a very good day to be in the very spot they were in.

Chapter 13

They did various times and ten trips through time that day. They checked and rechecked the squirrel, all the monitoring they'd done before and the videos taken while in transit. It was only about 4:30, so Tom decided he should do one more test; a human trial.

They all agreed they were ready for it, but if something happened and Tom wasn't on the walkie-talkie when the flyover happened in the morning, someone would be dropping from that helicopter for sure. He was too valuable for the first test. It needed to be one of the students, and it couldn't be Denver or Margaret since they had worked with the government. It had to be one of the other students that wouldn't be as easily missed. He was devastated, but knew they were right, as much as he wanted to be first, he couldn't jeopardize the whole mission if something did go wrong. Tom looked at George and said "Well Flash Gordon are you ready to be the first time traveler? I do believe you volunteered for that when I told you you'd been picked for the team." George leaped in the air, high fived anyone he could reach and exclaimed "You bet I am! I can't believe I get to be first! This is amazing. Folks I believe we've just moved up to first class status in this here experiment." They all laughed but each one wished it could have been them. They knew their time was coming and they'd just have to wait for it.

They pre-set all the coordinates and proceeded to get things ready. There didn't seem to be any undue stress on the squirrel, maybe because he wasn't going anywhere other than the future of the exact place he was leaving, so George should be safe if they did his test the same way. After they knew if humans could stand the transport, they'd start experimenting with traveling long distances from their current location. The squirrel survived six feet, but that was a very small test in the whole scheme of things.

They didn't have a formal craft built yet for George to sit in, so they strapped him to a chair and attached all the monitors, cameras, GPS, and controls to it. It would have to do this time. Then they'd get busy on some sort of vehicle to travel in.

They set everything to send George twenty minutes into the future and started the one minute countdown. Final checks were made and everyone was behind the lead barrier when Tom activated the power. Eighteen seconds later, the fog and ooze appeared and then in a flash of light, George was gone. "This is going to be the longest twenty minutes in history." Tom exclaimed. He sat down and waited, just like the rest of them. It was all they could do...wait.

Tom was still staring at the spot George departed from when he reappeared exactly twenty minutes later and started unhooking himself so he could jump up and down. He grabbed Tom and hugged him. Man what a thrill! Oh and there's a bear coming this way. He'll be here in about three minutes. He's big so we need to grab some stuff to make noise with to scare him away.

Could he see you? Are you visible in the future? Tom asked. "I don't know. He didn't pay any attention to me, so I might have been invisible, but he wasn't real close either. Maybe because I sat real still, he didn't notice me. I can't say for sure. I think we'll have to test that with a trip into the past. Someone can transport back a couple minutes to see if any of us see them. We will need to know that for protection during our travels.

They scrambled to grab some pieces of metal to bang together to scare the bear away and were ready when he walked into the clearing. He looked their way once and moved on. He didn't seem interested in them at all. They weren't a danger or enticing either. He probably smelled the berries just down the trail. George was jumping again, "See I told you. I told you it would be here and I was right on the money with the time too! I knew if something didn't spook him, it would take him about that long to get to me from where he was. Whew, what a rush! I really want to do it again. I want to be able to go into the future and be able to leave the chair and look around, then come back and set the time to travel back to our present." Tom explained that would be a few trials down the road, but they would be testing that. They had to be free of their chair in order to make changes in the past and check out those changes in the future. George knew it couldn't be right now, they all did, but they were so excited. It was really happening and it was getting more exciting by the minute. As each one's turn would arrive, that person would be giddy with excitement and anticipation.

Jody was excited and decided he really needed to get busy on the vehicle they'd be using for their traveling. He may have to park it in the future and finish it there once NASA wasn't snooping around so much, if that time ever came. He explained he was heading back to camp to work on it. Ryan decided he'd go with him and help hold things so Jody could make the connections. It would be hard to align the bracing and such all by himself, with no clamps or anything. They worked well together and knew this would be another project well completed with their joint efforts.

What they hadn't thought about until George came back was a test where he didn't come back in time, but time caught up with him. If the person stayed where they were in the future, would time just catch up with them and they'd reappear where they left, or would they continue living in their new time and never rejoin the real time they'd left? It was an interesting thought and they all presumed the person would just stay in that time and always be living in the future. If there were time travelers already, that would explain why there were gaps in people's lives, where it seemed they just dropped off the face of the Earth and then years later, just came back. That really sounds like a government experiment, but they couldn't have that technology or they wouldn't be funding this project. Hmmm, unless a different branch of the government had it and wasn't sharing. Now that made sense. Oh the conspiracy theories; but they were pretty believable considering the things the world has found out that were really true and unbelievable.

Since George had no issues, Tom told them he absolutely had to go next and it needed to be now. They laughed and helped set up the next configuration of date, time and equipment. Tom was going to be gone an hour, but was going to return to the time he left, so they would see him go and within the minute, he'd be back. That way they wouldn't be late getting back to camp. Everything went perfectly, the usual fog, the gooey ooze, the flash of light and then no professor. They stood watching in awe as they had every trip and in less than a minute he was back. He had adjusted the time while he was there and moved to another place and time that he didn't tell them about. He was not seen in the future until he exited his chair. He wasn't sure how that happened, but there seemed to be some sort of cloak around him and everything he had with him and it was in-tact, until he separated from the equipment; thus breaking the boundaries. (They really needed to get a vehicle of some sort made and give it a name, they didn't want to be like the squirrel and travel in a box or a chair. Although the box they were traveling in was merely a chair with everything strapped to it; it would protect them from anything that may be at the landing spot at the time of arrival.) He wanted to be able to control their experiments as much as possible, but when he was traveling, he had a ton of research to do, so it would require much traveling. He was actually gone three hours but returned to real time in the same minute he'd left. That was the dream of it all. He'd missed less than a minute of what was happening at "home", but had lived a full three hours in the future; and not in just one spot or time. His heart was pounding, but not from anything that happened during the traveling it was because of the excitement he felt at knowing his life's work was a success.

Tomorrow would be a full day of testing with everyone getting a turn at traveling, but also everyone would be working on their projects to hide everything from NASA. Those things were going to take some time as well. Once each piece of the puzzle was completed, Tom was going to take that piece with him and secure a storage building in the future, and begin storing everything there. He didn't want anything tangible laying around for anyone to see, should there happen to be someone drop in to check on them and their progress.

They kicked around the idea of Jody and Ryan going into the future to finish the vehicle, so it would be easy for them to get axles, wheels and tires to put on it. If Tom got the storage unit, then they could transport directly into it, then go get whatever they needed from torches to more metal. Tom figured a go-cart type frame would be sufficient for the body. They could bolt on all the equipment wherever it would be easy to access.

Tom did notice that every time they traveled it drained some energy stored from their initial boost. For example, they would be sent via the plutonium and tachyon pulse, then they could travel four or five more times from the energy they'd gathered to travel the first time. Continuous travel would require a power source, or at least a holding cell that could contain much more power than was being stored in the batteries of the equipment. This meant coming back to the original boost or developing a fuel cell that could last for years or be able to rejuvenate itself. Coming back to this place and time would work, as it was a constant and the power source would always be there, but if they could come up with something so that wouldn't be necessary; that would be the best solution. They'd have to be extremely careful not to change anything in the past that would change the spot where they could get power to travel. If they did, they'd be stuck in the future or past, whenever they happened to be when they ran out of power. He was going to talk to Denver about that since he'd already developed the cells NASA was using. They really needed something renewable because returning to this spot every time would be dangerous in that they could be caught. They needed to travel spontaneously and to different locations and only returning to the place they left for that particular leap.

He also thought that maybe the vehicle they were going to use for travel, might ought to look more like a real vehicle. Enclosed and comfortable so it would be disguised and not stand out in the future or past. They might need to buy a real vehicle in the future and modify it to contain the time travel equipment. He'd take a poll on that later to see what everyone thought would be best and alert Jody and Ryan not to proceed until he got the car.

They also needed to test traveling with two or more people in the vehicle, traveling with a trailer hooked to the back, or stuff on the roof. It should all work without any problems; but he wanted to make sure the power consumption wasn't an issue should the need arise to transport more stuff or a lot of people.

There were a lot of things coming up that they'd need to work out and they really needed to get busy on it all. Four months wasn't a very long time and they might not have that long. It would depend on how antsy someone got at NASA. Tom could tell it was going to be a long chat around the campfire that night. He knew they'd have all the answers, they'd just need to get them all out in the open and work out any bugs that came up. This many great minds working together was one of the more incredible parts of this experiment.

They gathered everything, secured what was left and headed back to camp for dinner and pow-wow.

They'd been provided with some pretty good food and the kids were really good cooks. It was almost gourmet and they were all loving it. It certainly wasn't college food.

Everyone was putting stuff away and gathering needed stuff for tomorrow. Some were cooking, some getting water and a couple headed for the showers so there wouldn't be a long wait later. Tom quickly found Jody and Ryan and told them not to work on the "box" any longer and told them to think about a real car to customize for their needs. "We getting a DeLorean Doc?" Jody laughed. Tom explained they didn't need speed, just a place to put everybody and everything they'd need in the car. Using a car instead of a go-cart would enable them to blend in better and also lock up from anyone noticing something they wanted to check out. He also suggested some tinted windows. They agreed and started thinking about what kind of car they should get. They told him they hadn't gotten very far, mostly just gathering stuff they thought they could tear apart and use. That was good, now nothing of NASA's would be destroyed except some equipment to leave enough evidence of an explosion and keep them in the clear for the instruments they were taking to the future.

Dinner was amazing, Steven had prepared lemon chicken, rice pilaf, steamed broccoli and even made fudge for dessert. Tom decided they could discuss their changes in needs while they ate and of course the main topic was a car. Jody was back to the '57 Chevy, any classic car would just be a cooler classic car in the future. They were real collector cars and people restored them. They also had a lot of room inside and a huge trunk. The glove compartment was very big and could conceal the coordinate boxes with date and time controls. They sometimes had a converter for fuel in them so there was a couple odd buttons on the dashboard they could swap out for the buttons they needed for time travel.

"Seems he's got a pretty good case doc and he's wanted to get his hands on one for years, so give the boy a break and let him have this one. Women love them too, so you may just be taking chicks out in your ride." Myra laughed. He agreed and Jody was in heaven!

The components are pretty common place as well, so I think we'll get the necessary stuff and build our own in the future so as not to have too much stuff go missing from NASA's inventory. They'll use a fine tooth comb, looking for stuff. We can build the tachyon pulse emitter as well and will only need the plutonium; or a chunk of it at least.

Tom explained they could work several hours a day in the future and get back here at the exact time they left so nothing would be out of order. They'd be tired doing so much work so fast, but they had to if they wanted to resume time travel as quickly as possible after NASA stopped grilling them about their failures. Everyone was more excited about everything. It just seemed that things were happening so fast for them and they couldn't tell anyone else, so their energy was just building up. Maybe doing a lot of manual labor would help them burn up some of that energy. They were all up for it, no matter how much sleep they lost, they'd chalk it up to exams. Everyone crammed for days and got very little sleep during finals, so it shouldn't be any worse than that; and this was SO much more important than finals. This would change the world.

Chapter 14

There was their wake up chopper! Margaret thought why, just why, can't they once be late. She along with everyone else started scrambling to get everything done and ready to start their traveling.

Tom had a bank note that would mature in ten years, so he was going to the bank, ten years from then and cash it in to buy the needed supplies and to find a car. Wait a minute, he'd just go back to 1957 and buy the car, it would be amazingly cheap and he could transport a brand new one to the future that would just need the modifications and no restoring at all. Jody would be bummed about the no restoration, but he'd get over it quickly enough when he got behind the wheel of that little beauty. He'd still need cash to get the rest of the supplies they'd need and pay five years rental on the storage unit. Now Tom's brain was working and thoughts kept flying into and out of it at a very rapid pace, stuff he hadn't thought of, like no, he'd get two cars and they'd make two machines, once the first one was operative, they would use it to travel while they were working on the second one. They could go four or five at a time in the Chevy versus two in the chair and that wasn't even comfortable. He was afraid to take more than six of the group at any given time because of being found missing. He and Denver would need to scout out a new place to come back to in the Chevy. He didn't want someone from NASA to show up while they were gone, thinking they'd taken a hike and have them appear in a nice new '57 Chevy in front of their eyes. They wouldn't be able to hide it then.

He would find a military surplus store too and get some camo netting to cover it with so it wouldn't be spotted in the middle of the woods. There really was a lot to consider when you were trying to hide something; especially from such thorough snoops as the government.

Alan decided he wanted to fix breakfast that morning, opting for an additional turn as he wanted pancakes and bacon. Everyone easily agreed and he set to work. It didn't take long, he sure seemed a pro with the griddles. He was entertaining to watch and with fresh blueberries and strawberries, they tasted amazing. Alison helped him clean up since he'd taken her turn cooking and they were done in a flash.

"Off to the future!" Myra exclaimed as they began their trek off to the clearing for today's experiments.

They were talking along the way about personal stuff, but when they arrived at the clearing Tom told them he wanted to try splitting up. He wanted to leave a couple at the mall, so they could buy tools, while he and Jody went to 1957 to get the car. When they brought the car back, they'd pick them up at the mall and proceed to the storage unit. He was afraid that might be all they could do without another power boost. They hadn't tested to see if weight were a factor in power usage. The Chevy was considerably heavy for a car even, and if power to weight ratio was a variable, then they'd probably have just enough for a trip home to recharge and then retrieve the others that were left. He told Myra they'd be gone about eight hours future time, but would be returning to the launch site about ten minutes after they left. He was really afraid to stay gone very long in real time as the potential for visitors increased every day they were there. He was also going to start returning about a hundred feet away in another, much smaller clearing, so if anyone should happen to be there, he wouldn't be spotted coming back from the future. Myra thought that was a great idea and suggested they put a squirrel in a box on the launch site, so they'd think they were gearing up for another experiment. It might be wise to build another squirrel box with everything needed for time travel attached—identical to the first one. It would be a back-up for them, but would also be at the ready once they left in the event someone else showed up. It seemed like Myra was thinking an awful lot about an unexpected visitor as well and didn't want anything ruining their plans. As a doctor, she'd seen plenty of stuff go on that shouldn't have and had even glimpsed a couple experiments that should have never happened with government idiots trying to build the perfect weapon using a soldier and lots of "other" parts.

Everyone had their checklists. The ones staying were going to work on duplicating the control boxes, in case of emergencies at the camp. Of course they would only have time to get the materials out, because the rest of the team would be back in ten minutes; and those going were getting the cash first, two cars, tools, jacks, pads to lay on under the cars, a storage unit, bolts, bracing, and the components needed to build duplicates of the control boxes for the future. They'd also need to pick up monitors, cameras and recording devices so they could document everything for posterity or reconstruction should the need arise in the future. Tom figured they wouldn't have much left over after he got all the stuff on the list, but it wouldn't matter, he'd go into the past and make an investment to cover all the costs they were about to incur. This was a beautiful plan and so easy to change your life when you could go back and do things differently or fix things you did wrong. He just needed to remember that changes had to be small. Buying fifty shares of Microsoft, Google, or Facebook would amount to a lot of money in just a few years and now was the few years it would be, so he'd have what he needed. He had to be very careful of any spending that he did, so as not to bring it to anyone's attention.

They were all working together and using their heads to do things the best, fastest, and cheapest way possible, like going into the past to get a $32,000.00 car for $2,600.00 and in perfect condition because it had just rolled off the assembly line. Now that was pretty sweet.

Myra gasped, they'd forgotten clothing for 1957. Once they'd traveled the ten years into the future, they'd look poor, but in 1957, they'd really stand out if they didn't have proper clothing on. Margaret suggested they find a vintage clothing store and Jody and Tom could change before they left for 1957. It's slip-ups like this that can cause problems and get them noticed in any era they were in. They really had to start thinking outside the box when it came to time travel. There were so many things that could go wrong or trip them up and get them caught.

Jody and Tom got to have lunch at a malt shop in 1957. They loved it all, the cars the music, the clothes, the innocent times when everyone was your friend and neighbor. People took care of one another and were friendly all the time. It was a good reminder that the work they were doing might just one day help the whole world to be like these folks were.

It was tricky getting both cars back. Tom and Jody put the chair inside the Chevy and brought it back. Jody took the chair out and he went back in the past to get the other Chevy. He then put the chair in that car and brought it back.

While they were in the past, Margaret and Ryan went to the mall in the future to get all the supplies they needed for everything else. Once they were back from the past, they drove to the mall and picked up all the stuff and their cohorts in time travel. Then they checked their power and were still good. It seemed like the trip itself was the only drain, they could have brought back twenty ton of equipment and it wouldn't have used any more power. Once they had everything in the unit, they began their trips back home. Tom told them he truly liked the trips with Margaret on his lap better than the ones with the guys. He knew Margaret was way too young for him, but at least she was a girl! They all laughed. Once they started using the cars it would be much easier to travel. It would be safer and more comfortable too. When they got to the smaller clearing, Tom told Margaret to wait until they all got back and then they'd head for the clearing together in case they weren't alone. It took three trips to get everyone back, and when they were all together, he told them he was getting really anxious about getting caught; so that's why the extra precautions were being taken. He also briefed everyone on the fact that if they did get caught, they would not turn on the tachyon pulse so the experiment would fail. They would have to explain every experiment anyway but they were leaving out the part about that combination working.

The four of them had had a very busy eight hours, but didn't seem too tired when they returned. Maybe the time travel rejuvenated them as they were going back to where they left. Tom felt had they stayed in the future; they'd have been tired after all their errands and organizing everything in the unit. They had everything set up in different areas, so they'd be able to work on the things they needed to build. With all the work areas ready, the supplies, and the car inside, they even had room to spare.

Next trips they made they were going to buy clothes at the vintage store; at least what was needed for Tom to travel into different era's and totes to put the clothes in to store in the unit.

For now, Tom wanted to let Denver and Alan take a trip to the future to work on the control boxes there. Alison was going to work on uploading everything to the USB drives for everyone to hide in their futures and then erasing the final data from the main system. Margaret was going to film more failed experiments with the squirrels so they'd have plenty of stock footage for the files. She had to change the date on the computer every time she made one so the files would all be on different dates and times. Then when she was finished for the day, she'd change the date and time back to current in case anyone came snooping. Tom,

George, Steven, Ryan and Jody were all going to work on the duplicate control boxes for this time.

Everyone was busy as they could be and Margaret was calling one of them over at a time to be the set-up person for that experiment, so she'd have five experiments for any given day and not duplicate clothes. She'd have them all change later and film five more to use for another day. She planned on doing this for ten days to give her twenty days' worth of failed experiments. She made sure she documented what each person wore and what date they did the experiment so she wouldn't slip up on something as simple as clothing. Most would just not work, but she'd have to do four or five with exploding squirrels. Seemed rather cruel, but no one complains about how many lab mice or rats get destroyed. At least her squirrels were killed instantly and couldn't feel much pain. She'd reuse as much of the footage as possible so to limit killing the squirrels and cleaning up the area. It was pretty yucky as it was spread over quite a big space.

Alison finished her work just about the time the boys returned from the future. She wanted to go hide hers since she hadn't gotten to travel into the future yet; and neither had Myra or Steven. Tom told her since she had stuff ready, she could go, but he really wanted her to take Steven with her. They agreed and since Steven knew where he wanted to hide his, they took off. They would be back in about ten minute's real time.

Alison sat on Steven's lap and they headed for their spots. They would know each other's, but just an idea, there were no street or city signs to tell them

exactly where they were. They might recognize the building if they were brought there, but that's all. The GPS was designed to only remember the last destination. Tom was too afraid someone would get their hands on it and know where they'd traveled to from the beginning and their efforts at change could all be undone if that happened.
It was exhilarating for them both. They were very careful not to get too excited and scream or yell as they were on a mission and didn't need to call attention to themselves; but as soon as they returned, they'd be whooping it up. This was incredible! They both sneaked a quick look at the newspaper at their own locations, just for the headlines. They were so curious about what was going on in the future, even if it was just a few short years away. Alison was glad to see her family was still safe and healthy.

Steven checked out his family and the headlines. He secured his USB card in a place he'd hidden stuff for years. He was the only one who knew about the small metal box he'd hidden in the attic, under a floorboard in the corner. He placed it in a plastic box, so a mouse wouldn't move it or anything should one chew through the floor, and secured it safely with his baseball cards and a couple rare coins his grandfather had given him. He smiled at the memories and hurried on his way before anyone came home and caught him there. That could be tragic, or would it?

"Alison, I have to make another stop!" I need to say goodbye to my grandmother. I didn't get to before she died and I want her to know what we've accomplished and that I love her and it wasn't my fault I didn't come. She'll be so proud of us all and will take it to her grave so no harm can come of it. PLEASE!?" he asked. She agreed and they zoomed off to the hospital the day before and at the time his family would have just left for the night before his grandmother's passing. He went in to see her, the nurse recognized him and didn't say anything about him being late. He asked her not to tell his family he'd made it, they'd just be upset at his long drive from school and he was just staying a few minutes before heading back home. She smiled and told him his secret was safe with her. She also explained that his grandmother hadn't been responsive all day. He entered her room and sat in the chair next to her bed. "Mamaw, I'm here." Was all it took for her to open her eyes and smile. "I've been waiting." She told him. He knew she would have been and he also knew she wouldn't have understood why he wasn't there. "I can't stay, but I wanted you to know how much I love and respect you." "I know Steven, don't you worry about me, I'll be just fine. I'll get me a new heart when I get to Heaven and it will be tonight. I'd have already been gone, but I was waiting for you to come. I knew you would. Now you go on back to school, I'll be leaving tomorrow. I'll see you again little one." She squeezed his hand and smiled again, then drifted off to sleep. It was so good to hear her voice again and to know she would be able to die without wondering why. He hurried back outside to Alison and told her she didn't have a clue how much it meant to him what she'd let him do. She just smiled, patted his arm and told him they'd better get back.

They set the coordinates and reappeared in the small clearing seconds later. Just as Alison removed herself from his lap, he remembered something vitally important. He asked her to wait a second and told her he just remembered his mother had told him at the funeral that when they got to the hospital the next morning, his Mamaw had said he'd visited her that night and she was ready to go on home now. She told him that his Mamaw must have been dreaming about him and she was at peace because she'd seen him. He had always thought that too, but now he knew, it's because he really was there. "Oh my Alison, do you know what this means? We really can change history and people's lives. Something as simple as me coming to her and telling my Mamaw I loved her, totally changed her life. It was only for a few hours in her case, but she died happy because of what I did just a few minutes ago. I'm going to get a chewing out for the detour, and I'll take full responsibility, but I have to tell Tom. It's too big not to. I'll tell him you didn't know until I got there." You don't have to cover for me. I was a willing participant in it all. I'll take the chewing out right along with you Steven. It was worth it." She smiled and squeezed his hand. He squeezed hers right back and took off running, pulling her along as he ran.

They were out of breath when they reached the clearing and everyone looked up in surprise. "What's chasing you all?" Tom asked as they came to a halt. "Nothing, but I have something to talk to you about. Can I tell everyone, or do you want to hear first and then enlighten everyone else?" he asked. "You may as well tell us all at one time, since Alison already knows and I'll be hounded until I tell them anyway. We're a team and we have a bigger secret than yours we're keeping, I suspect." Tom smiled and motioned for them all to have a seat.

Steven filled them in on his side trip to see his grandmother and then what he'd remembered when he returned. They were all as excited as he was. It was amazing that it was so easy. Another reason they had to be so careful about what they did and said in another time. He understood that Steven's grandmother wasn't really able to tell anyone and that it had made her life good at the end and his mother happy to know her mother had felt peace as well; but they had to really be extra careful. What if she'd said something to the nurse and she told that he'd been there for real, there might have been complications within his family that changed something about his schooling and he wouldn't have gotten the education he had, thus not being on the team and time traveling at all. It was a very touchy thing and he wanted to make sure they were all very aware of anything they did while traveling through time.

They all agreed with Tom and were in total agreement about the cautions needed during travel, but were so happy for Steven as well that his grandmother died in peace knowing he'd come to bid her farewell on her journey.

Tom also told them that they could make these side trips, but to give someone the coordinates and plan of action. Just in case they needed rescued or if there was something they missed that may cause issues with their present time or impact the whole world, the others might catch it and thus prevent any catastrophes that may occur. Again they all agreed and felt that was a good course of action. Once the person returned any notes and the coordinates would be burned so no evidence could be found by those in authority that might be suspicious of their activities.

It was time to head back to camp for dinner and to get things ready for the next day. Everyone needed to give updates on where they were with their projects and see if there was anything they needed.

They each did their daily chores and dinner was cooking. The smell of the onions and garlic was overwhelming. "What are we having for dinner?" was on everyone's mind but Tom actually voiced it.

Margaret said they were having Tuscany chicken, angel hair pasta, salad and a blueberry cobbler. She had the stand-up log going with the iron skillet sitting atop and the cobbler baking inside. The sauce for the chicken was what was causing the stir. It was very Italian and was a thinner sauce. Margaret told them they could have it in bowls if they wanted and just mix the pasta in. They all agreed that would work for them and they were starving, just smelling it cooking. It took less than forty minutes for everything to be ready.

They each laid their notes by their plates and discussed their needs and plans over dinner.

There were two sensors, a light and some wire that they needed for the control boxes. They were nearly out of milk and another bag of nuts for the squirrels would be good too.

Margaret asked that none of them wear the same clothes for the next five days and since that's all the clothes they had, they wouldn't have laundry duty until that time was over so they wouldn't inadvertently wear the same thing. It would be in the laundry bin. Then everyone would have to pitch in and help get all the laundry caught up. She'd need them to do this for two weeks at least and if they could wear a shirt with different pants than last time; that would be even better. She'd have the list and they could all check to see what needed matched up and put their clothes in their totes already matched. It was important if they wanted to keep up the façade they were working on.

Alison had everyone's USB card ready for hiding, so those trips would be taken throughout the day tomorrow.

Everyone was supposed to get a chance today and all but Myra got to go. It would be a good time for her to pick up the stuff for medical kits for the Chevy's and then she'd need to make one for the chair they were using. Since they were buying what they needed in the future, she wouldn't have to fake a bear tearing up the camp and destroying a lot of the medical stuff. This was a much cleaner plan. Anything they didn't have to make up to fool someone was better. There's a chance someone would tell a different story, or a part differently than someone else and then they were caught.

Alan also didn't have to do an explosion to cover up supplies they bought for the control boxes.

It seemed they had all the bases covered for the cover up and very little would not be told exactly as it was. They were all happy with that plan as it was the truest and easiest for everyone to remember.

Chapter 15

Their six o'clock alarm clock chopper was right on time, as usual. Tom was on the radio ordering the supplies and everyone else was getting up, ready to start another day. They had it all planned out, so everyone could hit the ground running, so to speak. There wasn't a sense of urgency in this group. Precision was the key factor and precision was what scientists were all about.

Showers were being taken, breakfast was cooking, you could smell the bacon cooking and coffee brewing. Ah what wonderful aromas to add to the natural scents of the forest. It was a good day and a beautiful morning to be in the forest. They were all in good moods as their time traveling was going so well. Their only spot of gloom, if you could call it that, was that they couldn't tell anyone, not yet anyway; but that was a small price to pay in order to be a part of all this.

Steven's trip yesterday had given them all a lot to think about. Did they really want to make changes in their pasts or just use what they know and discover about the future to make their today a better place. To make the right job choices, the right investments and the right decisions about where to go with their knowledge and experiences. Did they want to alter their careers or just expound on what they were doing right now. This was exciting and could be the adventure that kept them happy for years. Every day could be re-lived, every happy moment could be repeated a thousand times a day. Every bad relationship could be ended before it began; but would these things cause them to be different people? They had that fear, because they all knew problems and trials are what strengthens people. If they were happy with who they were, would they want to be different, or just make arrangements to have the means to enjoy who they were. There were some big moral questions to ask themselves. If they helped a friend at the cost of an acquaintance, was that the right thing to do? Why did life come with so many questions and why did new discoveries come with so many responsibilities. Oh to be children again, who just did what made them happy and didn't know to care about anything else. But people learn at an early age that their actions have consequences. Even babies are not happy if mama's crying. They know something's wrong. They knew they were not God and they didn't try to be, but is that what they were doing or about to do? They were all very down to earth geniuses and were really very environmentally aware. They had great big hearts and wanted to change the world for the better for everyone, not just themselves. As long as they kept this attitude of questioning themselves, Tom thought they would be alright, but if greed or the hunger for power came into play the world may not be better off for their accomplishments in this beautiful wilderness area of West Virginia. It would be a shame for such horrible things to come from such a great place. He knew he'd need reminding and they would too, for the rest of their lives. Is it really for the good of all? That was the question they would have to ask themselves every time they stepped into a time traveling device.

Right now they were light-hearted and happy, so hopefully that would continue the rest of their lives.

Breakfast was over and lunchtime snacks were packed, everyone was ready to head to the clearing.

It wasn't her normal duty, but Margaret was feeling a little sorry for the squirrels since she'd been doing so much filming and knew she'd have to blow up a few of them. So she volunteered to feed and water them that morning. She had the fresh bag of nuts under her arm and a gallon of water in her hand. She wished they were tame and could be petted, but they'd bite, so she just had to take care of their needs and go on. She gave each one a double portion of nuts and spoke kindly to them as she put the food in and refilled their water bottles. She picked up sturdy pieces of branches as she walked and put one in each cage so they would have something to climb on other than just the side of the cages. She smiled as she left them, they seemed happy and she didn't feel quite so guilty.

George, Steven, Ryan and Jody were pulling out the stuff to work on the control boxes as Margaret headed to set up the computer for recording the experiments. Tom had just said he was taking Myra into the future and had been questioned about them both not being there should anyone come. He didn't care, he wanted to get his USB card hidden and so did she. They'd been friends a long time and he really wanted a little time alone to talk to her about any concerns she might have and to take her to dinner somewhere nice to say thanks for all her years of support. A sort of celebration. He also wanted to get a new bottle of champagne to replace the one they drank. That way there wouldn't be any speculation about how it got broken, etc. He'd gathered all the pieces of glass and put in a bag the day they'd broken it, but he hadn't put it in the trash, something just didn't seem right about that. Now he knew why, he'd leave the broken glass in the future. There was a trash receptacle by the storage unit and then he would replace the champagne in the present. No one would be the wiser. NASA would see there had been no reason for celebration, confirming their story. It was a good way to cover up everything.

He chose a time in the not so distant past and took her there for dinner. She gasped when they appeared at their destination and it was Paris in the springtime. He hid the chair and they strolled towards the Eifel Tower at sunset. They ate at the restaurant there and the view was incredible. He wasn't looking for romance or anything; he just wanted it to be special. She'd been there for him for years and couldn't have been a better friend. She thanked him over and over for the special evening and thoroughly enjoyed their decadent meal. He bought chocolates for everyone on the way back to the chair and then they went to hide their cards.

They'd been gone for hours in the future, but came back about a half hour later in real time. He wasn't sure why he didn't come back at the same minute just in case someone was there, or why he didn't just stay away for hours, but that's what he did. It had given the team a few minutes to talk amongst themselves about anything bothering them and how they felt about it all and what plans they had for changes they wanted to make. But it didn't give them long enough to start wondering or worrying about the professor and the doctor.

Myra thanked him again for dinner and the wonderful trip to Paris, told him he was a great guy and she appreciated his friendship as much as he did hers. They'd had a lot of years together and now it had all paid off. They'd accomplished what he'd wanted to for years.

The guys thought they would be able to have the control boxes finished by tomorrow and they could test simultaneous trips to see if the rift stayed open long enough for another vehicle to pass through if it were right behind the first one, but not touching. This may help them figure out if the rifts stayed open longer than the few seconds they thought. No one had ever just walked over to the spot to see if they could walk through it after the initial person went through. They were afraid that they might get lost in time if they weren't attached to a device containing the necessary control boxes. They already knew they could go through together, whatever was touching would go at the same time.

They also thought it might be good to see if the same emission of power and tachyons would send them both from two different locations. Close enough for the powers to be picked up and power each machine, but far enough apart for it to create two rifts.

The camp seemed quiet as everyone was engrossed in their own thoughts. It was like they were all trying to think of things to test and ways to move through time and still keep it all secret from the government. Margaret filmed a total of thirty five failed time travel attempts that day. She wanted to get a little ahead and everyone was around so she could get lots of people done. When she finished everyone, she sent them to change and started the round again. It was much faster this way, all she had to do was change the date and time when she started each one and she'd be finished with enough to give her a couple days break so she could do a trip or two with the others. Once Margaret was done for the day, they all called it a day and decided to have a little fun to take their minds off all the rush and pressure. They needed it.

Dinner would be hotdogs, cooked on sticks over the campfire. They all got busy and made some baked beans, potato salad, homemade sauce and slaw. They also had chips and yet again Alison produced supplies for s'mores. George got his guitar out and they all sang songs, laughed and talked more about their lives, families, likes, habits, and hobbies.

No talk of the government, NASA, the past or the future, they were living in the moment and the moment was good. They had good food, good company and a good outlook on the future. They were all ready to move on with the project and they were all well versed on their responses to anyone asking any questions, so they didn't have to think for a couple hours. They played a couple games, sang some silly songs and some serious songs. There was even a little dancing. For the first time in days, they were acting like typical college students and it felt good. Even Tom and Myra were fitting right in; the lighthearted mood did them all good.

Everyone did remember to retrieve their own clothes from the line and put away in their tents. Tomorrow would be another day and they could worry about the fate of the world then.

Chapter 16

Up with the chopper! Six o'clock and all was well. They could smell the sausage cooking and the coffee brewing. Another day another time to conquer! They were anxious for today. As soon as the control boxes were finished, they could begin multiple trips into time. They all seemed to be in a real hurry to get going, so things progressed quickly and they were all dressed, finished eating and heading for the clearing except for Alison and Alan. They took all the laundry and headed for the stream to wash clothes. She'd have done it all by herself, but where they'd done so much filming and a lot of physical work, there was an overabundance of laundry to be done and it got pretty heavy carrying all the wet clothes back to camp to be hung on a line.

When they arrived at the creek, Alan immediately strung a line across the creek and took a basket to the other side to work on, while Alison worked on the side closer to the camp. They washed in buckets with a minimal amount of soap so as not to harm the environment, rinsed in the creek, wrung as much water out of each item as possible, then tossed it across the line to begin dripping. This would also keep the clothes clean while they worked on the rest. Once all the clothes were washed, they worked together to wring as much water as possible out of each item. By each holding an end or side of the garment and twisting it, they could remove much more water than one person could do alone. They would dry much faster and be much lighter carrying back up the hill to camp. Once they were back to camp Alan started hanging the clothes on the line. Alison pulled each piece out, shook it good to help avoid wrinkles and handed it to Alan to hang since he was taller and they wanted it hung higher to catch any breeze blowing to help them dry.

After everything was hanging to dry, they sat down for a drink and a snack. They were sort of tired, it wasn't real hard work, but there was a lot of it!

They figured they weren't needed at the clearing yet, so they did a little prep work and put dinner on, so it would be ready when they all returned. They cut up vegetables and made pot roast. It would need to slow cook about five hours, and that's real close to what they had left before dinner. When they had it all together and simmering on their tree log stove, they headed back to the clearing to offer help with any project needing their attention.

They each collapsed into a chair when they got there like they were exhausted from all the laundry. Alison, in her most southern voice exclaimed her despair at being all hot and stick-eh doing all that manual labor and now needing to retire for respite and being forced to endure more work. It just wasn't fittin' for a la-dee of her importance. Margaret apologized and they all burst out laughing. They had decided to keep the pot roast a surprise until everyone got back. Alison was all about surprising people with food. She did love to cook, so that was probably why. They got up and started prepping an experiment for Margaret to film.

It was about four o'clock when they finished the

control boxes. It was tedious work and their shoulders ached from the detail work required and working in such small compartments. Myra promised hot packs for everyone when they got back and maybe a few shoulder massages too.

They called it a day and headed back to camp. The aroma of the pot roast hit them all about the same time and Ummm was the word on everyone's lips. Those not getting into the shower were treated to hot packs first. Once the heat nearly left the packs, Myra would massage the muscles and stretch their necks. They all felt much better and very relaxed for dinner.

Alan and Alison prepared some crackers and toast to go with the pot roast, fixed drinks, and they were delighted that it only took a few minutes for everyone to settle in for dinner.

They talked a while then the rest took their showers and everyone settled into their own thing, whether it be a book, the internet, or calling home to chat with family for a few minutes. They only had internet and cell service for three hours each evening as NASA's satellite was overhead and they'd been given codes to access it.

It wasn't long before the camp grew quiet as one by one, they went to sleep, hoping to dream of exotic places or times in history that they might travel to one day very soon. They each had special destinations they wanted to see and events they wanted to witness and now it would all become a reality. I's a wonder they could sleep a wink, even being physically exhausted from their day of hard physical labor.

Chapter 17

Well it was another exciting day at the camp. Most of them were awake when their helicopter alarm clock, as they like to say, went off at 0600 hours.

Breakfast was already cooking and people were showering and dressing rather quickly. They were excited because they knew they would be time traveling most of the day. They were so looking forward to it. They had eaten, gathered their supplies and were at the clearing an hour earlier than usual. It was good to share a common goal and interest with such a great bunch of people.

They decided to test travel from two separate but close locations first. They mounted all the equipment onto the second chair and put Jody at the helm. Steven was manning the original chair and the others were watching or manning the power sources. Now the power source was aimed at the original chair and Jody's chair was fifty feet to the left of it. The Tachyon pulse would not be limited to any sort of aiming, it would radiate 360 degrees for about a half mile. They aimed the plutonium and started the tachyon. Within five seconds the light flashed, the ooze appeared and both chairs left the clearing.

Now they sat wondering if this was a good thing or a bad thing. Nothing else seemed to go with it, even the leaves didn't seem disturbed, so it wasn't a problem on this end, but would it be a problem should someone in another craft be able to use your power if you didn't want them to and that seemed to be a definite yes. Again, not a problem in their hands; but in the hands of the government, that would be a different story. They could launch a fleet of travel crafts with one emission of power.

When Jody and Steven returned in their allotted two minutes, they decided to lower the power and try again. This time Ryan and Alison would man the crafts. They decreased the power by 50% and weren't even sure if it would be enough to create a rift or not, but it did and just as easily as the first time. The ooze and the fog were the same. They really couldn't tell a difference and they both did leave. Tom was getting excited to know the power required wasn't as much as they thought. This would make it easier to obtain in the future as well.

Next trip was with George and Alan, they decreased the power another 50%, so they were currently at 25% of original power. George went but Alan didn't. When George returned, they moved Alan's chair ten feet closer to the point the plutonium was aimed at and tried again. Again George left, but Alan was still sitting there waiting; so they moved him ten more feet and tried again and again. He didn't leave until he was within ten feet of the point of the power target. This was what they wanted. Someone would have to be very close in order to utilize the power designated for the first craft, or they'd have to be connected.

Next was Denver and Margaret's turns. They positioned Margaret to go first, then Denver would move his chair to her position to see if he could go through the rift on her power usage to open the portal. Tom was operating the stop watch to see if they could tell how long it was open.

Denver moved quickly to the spot, but ten seconds was too long, the portal was closed. They started him closer and got down to five seconds and he still could not go through. Finally Tom picked up a branch and as soon as they activated power and Denver went through the portal, he started the timer and then tossed the branch towards the rift. After three seconds the branch was suspended in the air, just hanging there. Another two seconds and it dropped. It didn't go through, so it was no longer suspended. "That was AMAZING Professor!" George exclaimed. They all cheered and talked about what a sight that was, just hanging in mid-air. The branch wasn't damaged and the whole thing fell, not just a piece, so if someone got trapped, it seemed they'd just be set free momentarily after the rift closed. So now they knew if someone were in the ten foot radius when the power started, they would immediately travel to the coordinates on their device; but someone walking by who entered the 10 foot radius would not go through the portal. However if someone not in the 10 foot radius could get to the exact spot the portal opened within ten seconds then they would transport as well. So fighter jets could enter after the tank went through, or a motorcycle or vehicle bearing down on the person leaving could transport within that timeframe and continue their pursuit of the person traveling. This was a very good thing to know in the event someone found out they could travel and were trying to catch them. They'd have to make sure they had enough space between them before they activated their traveling machine so as not to allow whoever was chasing them to follow into another place and time.

Oh Mr. Squirrel Myra called...he was about to gain his freedom. They put his cage right by the point he needed to be and used a string to open his door from a safe spot outside the ten foot radius, just as Myra and the chair departed. He shouldn't have enough time to exit real time and end up in the future; but should be caught in the closure if he ran out quickly, like they suspected he would. He did just what they expected and was caught in mid-air as he jumped to go through the hole. It had closed on him like it had the branch. After two seconds, he was dropped and seemed unharmed as he scurried away as fast as his legs would take him. HE WAS FREE! He'd earned his freedom too. His actions told them they would be safe should they be caught mid phase. Next up was George, Mr. Flash Gordon himself. He was going to attempt to walk through with the second chair, after Tom exited in the first chair. The plan was to make sure he wasn't harmed. He took a couple deep breaths and told Tom to go ahead and engage. As soon as they engaged the power, he started running the ten feet he needed to cover to reach the opening. It worked like a charm. He was suspended in mid step for two seconds. Myra rushed over to take his vitals and make sure there were no issues; and there were none! She also took some radiation readings and they were negligible. She'd already run tests on everyone's radiation badges and they were only being exposed to a bare minimum of radiation. That was a big worry off her mind as she was afraid they'd have residual effects from it and she didn't want this team of extreme intellectuals suffering unnecessary brain damage or cancer from their experiments.

Next test was to actually get through before the

rift closed. George said he'd go ahead and do that as well. He started running from fifteen feet just before they engaged so he was still a foot outside of the ten feet radius, but had enough momentum to make it to the rift before the three seconds. He went through perfectly and was back in a minute riding the chair this time. He was stoked! Of course they all loved perfecting the time travel, so that wasn't too surprising. They had to go through all this to make sure they didn't bring something or someone back when they traveled or allow someone or something to go behind them when they left and possibly be stranded in the past or future, depending on where the team member was traveling.

All these test also showed them that the power didn't actually decrease and stay used up because of the traveling, but seemed to regenerate itself once the traveling was over.

Tom decided it was time to remove the piece of plutonium they needed for their Chevys and they'd be ready to travel from the future at any time. He and Alan put on the lead aprons, got behind the lead enclosure, opened the case with the plutonium and took about three ounces. That should be enough to power their machines for a hundred years. They were hoping this little of an amount wouldn't be detected by NASA when they were putting stuff away, but it wouldn't matter, they had to have it. They built a container that could be aimed at a designated spot, like the one they had been using in their experiments, and placed the piece they took in it. Then they set up a
test to make sure that was enough power to send them on their way. Ryan and Alison were in the

driver's seats this time. It was certainly enough to power their travels. They built another container and separated it so half could be with each Chevy and they could power from within no matter where they may travel. Once separated they traveled again to be sure the even smaller amount was enough and it was, apparently it didn't take nearly as much as they'd thought originally. Tom made a mental note to do some further testing on that. If they could decrease the amount to the bare minimal power they'd need and it would also sustain itself for years then a scan for it would show trace minerals, but would not detect the plutonium. It would be much safer for them to have and use without being detected by anyone looking for it.

Since it was ready to go to the future, he sent it with Ryan to put in the Chevys. They would need to build another tachyon pulse emitter and each car would be completely independent in itself.

George said he and Steven could work on that the next day. It shouldn't take them more than a couple days to get it done. If they needed something for it, Denver or Ryan could go to the future to get it and they'd keep working. They all agreed it was a wonderful plan; and being self-sufficient would take away their dependence on anyone else, government or civilian.

It was all falling into place and it was mainly because this group of wonderful, smart, brilliant, dedicated, students worked so hard and felt the need to keep this a secret from "Big Brother". Tom only hoped they could get everything ready in the future before NASA started checking on things or sent someone to observe. He knew one thing for sure, if they sent someone to watch, there would be a lot of squirrels paying the price for it. He laughed to himself about that, but then felt a little sad for the squirrels. He didn't like wasting their lives and that would be somewhat of a waste since it would be an unnecessary evil due to the government's inerferrence.

They each took a turn going to their favorite place on Earth, whether it was an amusement park, the beach, or some restaurant, the sky was the limit. They deserved their mini vacation. They went in twos so they would have someone to enjoy themselves with. Tom's only instructions was to come back a minute after they left; and be sure to come back to the small clearing.

Once all their trips were over, they were all ready for dinner and bed. They weren't tired from their escapades in the future, they were tired from the extreme adrenaline running through their veins. They sat around the campfire and told where they'd each gone on their vacation. They all had a wonderful time and it was nice to get away. As much as they fed off each other and loved the work they were doing, there was still stress involved and those few hours were amazingly refreshing. Even just strolling along the beach settled the nerves, cleared the mind and refreshed the spirit. Tom sure knew about people and he hit this one right on the nose.

Those left behind during the vacations worked on their chores and stuff they still had to do to keep NASA appeased once everything was revealed at the end. There was still video needed for every day, so Margaret had that to work on. There was laundry to do, cooking of dinner, stuff to clean up, squirrels to feed. All the daily stuff they did. Those staying behind were looking forward to their turn and those returning were ready to tackle the world again. Since they were returning a minute after they left, it wasn't a long wait for the next person's turn. They'd barely gotten started on their chores when it was their turn then they only lost a minute before getting back to their chores again. It was crazy. If they weren't in the middle of it, and someone was just telling them, it would seem totally impossible, but with time travel it wasn't. It was sheer joy at being able to do so much in such a short amount of time. Actually a person could stay away for years living a totally different life and then return and only a minute would have passed since they had left their original life. That part was hard to wrap your mind around how time had to actually wrap around itself in so many different ways and levels in the same space they were occupying now.

Tom remembered the chocolates he had forgotten about getting for everyone in France until he returned from this trip, so he got them out and whipped up some amazing chocolate crepes for dessert that evening. It was only his second time cooking and this was just dessert, but they all loved them. He did remember to destroy all the wrappers in the fire. Chocolate from France would be a dead giveaway that they'd traveled in time.

Chapter 18

The helicopter arrived on time, but cautioned Tom about a storm moving in. It looked like it might be a rough one so they took every precaution with the gear and supplies, to make sure everything was put away and tied down. They dressed, had breakfast, and headed to the clearing for experiments.

They had been watching the skies and didn't see any evidence of a storm, so they'd decided to continue experiments until it started looking bad and they would quickly gather and secure those things and head back to camp. What they didn't realize was the fact that a storm moving in the direction it was, could not be seen until it was upon them.

They'd set up another time travel scenario where the two travelers would go to separate places and then meet up at another destination before coming back. They wanted to make sure all their equipment was working properly and synchronized to the hundredth of a second. Everything was a go and Alan had just hit the power button to send Steven and George into the future when a lightning bolt hit the ground behind them and thunder immediately followed it. The sky got pitch black in seconds, but it was too late for the experiment to be stopped—Alan had already hit the button. The ooze covered them, the fog appeared, the light flashed and both people strapped to their chairs disappeared. Once they were gone, everyone started shutting things down, securing the equipment and gathering the things they needed to take back to the camp. It had taken them about twenty minutes to get ready to go. Tom turned to scan the clearing once more before they headed out and that's when everything got very real, very fast.

He gasped when he saw the ooze and everyone else turned. They all saw it and the fog, then the familiar flash of light. Now no one disappeared because no one was standing there. The plutonium power had been flipped off with the crash of thunder and the tachyon was turned off immediately after that. So what caused the rift to open? Everyone looked at Tom and were all talking at once. What happened? Did you do something? How did that happen? Are we in danger? All valid questions being shouted out by everyone to Tom, maybe, but no one in particular, really. They didn't have but seconds to digest what had happened because just as suddenly as the first time, lightning struck and the thunder crashed. "To the trees!" Tom shouted above the roar. They all ran into the trees to avoid the lightning and the deluge of rain that followed it. It was less than a minute later that they heard the guys calling from the small clearing, asking was everyone alright. Tom shouted for them to come into the trees with them. Steven shouted back "We really need to take shelter from this rain, it's pouring and blowing in sheets against us." They could barely hear him, but Tom yelled again it was urgent for them to join them in the trees near the clearing.

It took them a few minutes to walk over there and he was explaining to them that the rift had reopened about twenty minutes after they'd gone. They were getting drenched, but they had to stay to see if it happened again.

As they checked their watches, they realized it must have been twenty minutes after the departure that it reopened, so if it were a repetitive anomaly, then in less than a minute it would reopen. They were right, twenty more seconds and it did it again; at exactly the twenty minute mark the rift reopened again on its own. This time they were all standing solid, just staring at the ooze, fog and light.

"What in the world! Who went through in this raging storm?" George exclaimed. "NO ONE!" Tom shouted again to be heard over the sound of the beating rain and thunder. The storm was on top of them, but they couldn't leave. They needed to know if anything or anyone went through that rift when it opened. He explained to the guys about the storm and the rift opening itself repeatedly at twenty minute intervals. This was a pure disaster of the greatest magnitude.

Alan and George decided to run to the camp and get a couple tarps to give them some shelter and as soon as the storm calmed enough that they could hear each other, they'd need to brainstorm what had happened. Tom agreed and they did just that. They also grabbed a few blankets, wrapped them inside a tarp to keep them dry, pulled on their own rain suits and got back as quickly as possible. They told everyone to stoop down as they were going to hang the tarps low and at a slant to keep as much rain out as possible and the water flowing down the slope, off the back. Once the first two tarps were hanging between four trees, and everyone was under them; Alan opened the last tarp and handed out blankets for them to use to dry off with and the rest to wrap up in as this rain had chilled them to the bone. They moved to the side nearer the front so George and Alan could spread the last tarp on the ground for them to sit on and huddle up against the cold. They were both soaked as well, long before they put their rain suits on, but they didn't get any wetter on the way back. They both removed their suits and dried as best they could as well. By the time all this was done, the storm had eased up. It seemed the eye had passed and they were just getting some hard rain by then. They watched for the lightning and then listened for the thunder and found the storm was almost two miles away now. The rain was slowing, but the rift was still opening every twenty minutes. They could hear each other now, if they spoke a little loudly. They no longer had to scream, so they decided to re-examine the whole scenario.

Everyone recounted their exact memories of what had happened before and after they'd sent Steven and George into the future. Neither of them had noticed anything strange or different during this trip. They did see the lightning and hear the thunder as they left, but otherwise the trip was unremarkable.

The main consensus was either there was too much power, due to the lightning giving a boost of energy as it struck at very close range, or the barometric pressure was a factor, since the storm was right on top of them.

There had been high pressure days since they were there, but nothing like this. They were literally a few hundred feet from the bulk of this storm as it topped the mountain and was passing right over them. It was a guessing game and they'd have to come up with a way to re-enact it to see if they could recreate the repeat effect again. But they really needed to figure out how to stop it for now.

Tom wanted to caution everyone not to get too close to the coordinates of the rift because they may get sucked through and without a control box attached to them, they would have no way of returning. They only had two control boxes, so anyone closer than fifty feet would need to be sitting in or attached to one of the chairs. Not that it had worked closer than ten feet, but they couldn't take any chances, something had changed and they didn't know at this point if it could enlarge itself as it gained momentum or if it would die out due to lack of power. One thing for sure they all knew they had to watch it and be very careful of getting too close, just in case there were issues they didn't know about yet.

Steven asked if they had a way to test or measure the power from the plutonium. If so, they could force pressure around and on it to see if its power magnified. Tom told him that was a great idea and with a couple adjustments, since the rain had passed, they could test that theory. This would tell them if the barometric pressure could have caused a change in the power level or not. He and Steven got right to work on that and within twenty minutes they were conducting the test. Unfortunately no amount of pressure placed on the plutonium changed it at all; it still gave out the same amount of power. At least they knew it wasn't that. Now to test what affect the pressure might have on the tachyon pulse. They'd have a few adjustments to make, but it would work almost the same way. After about ten minutes, they knew the atmospheric pressure had nothing to do with the rift, as far as they knew, or could tell anyway.

They'd have to figure out what did cause it and how to fix it before NASA showed up in the morning. Flying over, they'd have to have their eyes shut not to notice the light from the rift opening up.

Ryan had been very quiet for a few minutes before this and when he finally spoke, he explained that his calculations showed at every twenty minutes, the rift would be opening right about the time the chopper was arriving to the camp, it would be impossible for them not to see it. They needed to use the tarps, leaves, branches and debris to see if they could build a makeshift camouflage covering for that area that would shield the light from above. They needed to get busy and build this right away. If it worked, it would buy them time to figure out how to seal the rift.

Margaret had set up the camera and started recording as soon as the rain stopped. She had been watching the rift as well so they would know if there were an animal that had passed through or if anything else had as well.

Denver suggested he should get in the chair, use the same coordinates he'd used when he left and check out the future to make sure nothing was wrong there and to watch to see if the rift was opening on the other side. If so, he'd reset his coordinates and reenter by being on the spot when the twenty minutes were up. They all agreed that was a splendid idea too. If it was open from that side, they'd need to make sure nothing or no one came through to their side. He was gone and back in a flash. Nothing irregular from that side and he'd stayed a good half hour in the spot he arrived in, so if there were an anomaly on that side, he'd be caught up in it. He also reported that nothing felt or looked different as he was transported to the future. That was a good thing to know as they sure didn't want something or someone coming from that side back to them.

Jody grabbed the tarp ropes and rubbed them in the mud and rubbed a lot of mud into the tarps as well. He wanted to camouflage them. He then drug them through the leaves and the tarps were covered pretty good by that time. He felt they were ok, so he started cutting four saplings from the wooded area to hold the tarps high above the spot so they wouldn't get sucked into the rift. He'd asked Ryan to go get some more rope, the white cotton kind would camouflage best, so that's what he brought, then immediately began rolling it in the mud and leaves. Once ready he and Jody affixed the tarps corners to each of the trees. They were slanting the poles from the middle out to the top so they couldn't be seen from above, but not so much as to lower the covering too far down towards the rift. It looked like it was going to hold and Jody so wished he could see it from above to know if it was good enough or not. It looked good on the ground, so he was going to presume it looked good off the ground.

Once the rift reopened, they watched. First good thing was it didn't take the tarps into the future, so they knew you had to be very close to the spot in order to travel with it. Second good thing was they couldn't see the rift's light coming out on the sides, so they probably wouldn't be able to see it from above. It worked and Jody was so glad, as was the rest of the team.

Well that bought them some time, but they were really no closer to finding out how to stop it from happening than they were an hour ago. It was still very consistent and opened exactly every twenty minutes.

Next thing was to check to see if the amount of power from a bolt of lightning could amplify the power enough to cause a repeat effect. They had to calculate the power from the lightning bolt and add that to the power from the plutonium and then figure out what to use as the additional power source to recreate the same amount used during the anomaly that started the rift to opening repeatedly on its own. It took a couple hours and all eight of them calculating to decide on a number of kilowatts needed to replicate the original burst of power that was emanating during the time travel send-off that started all this mess. Once they were all in agreement, they tried the experiment again. It worked and sent Margaret into the future, but it did not replicate the issue at hand. However the rift was still opening right on schedule.

They all sat down rather defeated and looked at each other for more ideas. Unfortunately they had none at the moment.

It was getting late so Tom suggested they go back and have dinner. Denver said he'd take the first watch since they had to make sure nothing went through from this side and still monitor the times it opened in case that happened to change. They said someone would come get him shortly and they'd stay while he went back, ate, showered and cleaned up from all the rain, mud and gunk he'd gotten all over himself.

It wasn't too long before Alison came back, looking all fresh and well fed. She was carrying a chair to sit in and her water bottle. She told him it was hot, so he could eat first or shower first, whatever was best for him and then hit the hay for at least four hours before coming to relieve her.

After they'd all had dinner, they started cleaning up the debris that was scattered around the camp, bagged all the dirty clothes for the laundry run in the morning and cleaned up the dishes, chairs and equipment boxes. Then Alan grabbed a dry tarp from the box and went to make camp for him and Alison. When she got sleepy, he'd watch and by the time he got sleepy, Denver should be coming back after his four hour sleep to relieve him. They could decide who would be next, but they'd have to have their campsite cleared before six in the morning. There would be no explainable reason for any of them to have slept out there all night. They had to keep everything unquestionable!

Alison was asleep and Alan was deep in thought about everything when Denver arrived to relieve him. He told him there was no change and went to warm his back against Alison's back on the tarp. It had gotten a little chilly and bless Denver's heart, he'd brought two blankets for them to use. That boy thought of everything.

Denver woke them up in time to clear up their things and head back to camp before the chopper arrived. He would stay close to watch the rift, but he'd stay out of sight. They could bring him some breakfast when they all came back to work on figuring out what to try next. Alan and Alison thanked him and headed off with everything in their camp, assuring him someone would be back very shortly to give him a break.

Chapter 19

Well the chopper came and went with no issues, so they all breathed a little better, but back to the issue at hand. No one said anything about it while getting dressed, cooking and having breakfast, but it was in all their thoughts. Tom was the first to speak and he was expressing his exasperation at the whole thing, when Alan yelled "I've got it!" He explained to them that all he needed to do was travel back in time to just before the storm hit and they were sent into the future. Back to just before whatever happened that caused the rift. He could tell them to stop the experiment and why. No original experiment, no rift.

It was certainly worth a shot so they gathered their stuff, fixed Denver a plate, and headed towards the clearing. Denver ate and said he was good and would stay with the group. He really didn't need any sleep at the moment.

They got the experiment set up and waited for Alan to get back from the past. If it went well, there would be some immediate changes in their surroundings. Like the camo canopy would be gone, since it wouldn't have been needed had the test not gone awry.

Denver got back, said he'd persuaded them not to do the experiment, but it didn't seem to have stopped the rift. It opened while he was still in the past and was about to open in their real time in just a couple minutes. They had proceeded to do everything like they were doing the first time around. It didn't make any sense at all.

What could have caused the rift if it wasn't their experiment. They opened the rift to begin with and normally it closed right behind them within three seconds. They'd tested that theory and found if they immediately went through, they could; but if they waited just a few seconds it would be closed and they couldn't use it for another trip on the same power expended.

He told them he didn't know what to say or do, he'd stopped the experiment, but the rift was still functioning. And by the way, he said, it was creepy seeing yourself face to face like that.

Alan suggested he, or someone, pass through the rift that was about to reopen and see if it was still depositing them in the same place as originally set.

Maybe the only way to seal the rift was to pass through it with whatever it took to seal it and of course they had no clue what that would be yet. Maybe they had to be at that exact place and pass from the other side. They were just suppositions being flung out. So they agreed to try that. He was to go into the future at the point the first rift happened and come back through it to the now past and see if that changed anything.

None of it made sense, but they were very willing to try anything and everything to repair this damage to the time continuum. They had no clue what damage this might cause in the future. While Alan was gone this time, they talked more about what they thought might seal the rift. They'd kicked around so many ideas and none of them had worked; they were grasping at straws, but they had to have a place to start, a different angle to look at it and something to help them feel not so useless. Any suggestion was a good one until they tested it and proved it not the one that would work for this situation. Any comment could spark the thought in someone else that would lead to the solution. Tom told them if anything and he meant anything popped in their minds, don't hesitate to share it, even if it sounded ridiculous. After all time travel seemed ridiculous to most people and they knew it was possible as they'd all done it. He explained that voicing it aloud would register it in everyone's mind and something may just come of it after all. This wasn't elementary school when people had to be afraid to speak up, this was a meeting of the greatest minds of their generation and Tom meant every word of that. He held them in highest regard and was honored to have them all there and that affection had grown after working with them for just this short amount of time.

Ryan suggested that maybe the time particles that seemed to fall out each time they opened the rift could be collected and put back into it to seal it. Maybe there were too many lost and it couldn't hold itself together any longer.

Alan came back from the past and going back through from the back side (or future) didn't fix it. They told him Ryan's idea and he said it sounded feasible to him, but how could they collect the time cells? Surely they'd fallen apart, rotted, or however time cells went to waste. Otherwise there would be a big pile of them lying around. They disappeared quickly after they saw them fall. Maybe they'd opened the portal in the same spot too many times. They knew for sure to move at least fifty feet away for the next experiments. They didn't know how to collect the cells, they could feel them on their skin, but when they went to wipe it off, it was gone. It almost acted like it was water. When a few drops of water dropped, it would evaporate quickly and not be noticed any longer; especially if it landed on the ground.

So they decided to go looking for some sort of residue on the ground where the time cells had fallen. They took flashlights to help them see and thought possibly it might show a reflection, glint or glimmer of sorts if it were still wet. They expected them to be gone, unless they couldn't be diluted with water, because of the torrential rain they'd had, but everything was worth investigating. They had to find a way. They searched several minutes then realized it was just two minutes before the next opening, so they all backed away from the spot. They didn't have control boxes so they might be lost in time somewhere and definitely didn't want that happening; at least not by choice anyway. It was sort of a romantic thought to be lost somewhere you really wanted to be so you could live that life doing something you really loved to do, or being with someone you loved and they were gone too soon.

Ok, so immediately after the rift opened and closed everyone wiped at their faces, skin and clothes to see if they could capture any time cells. They also took off running toward the rift to see if they could catch any right at the source. There really wasn't anything to speak of. Maybe it was being absorbed into their skin. That stuff had to be going somewhere and right now it was their only hope of sealing the rift.

"Steven, you're the particle expert in our group. Do you think we could figure out what it is and fabricate a glue to hold it together?" Myra asked. "Well, I'm not sure." He said thoughtfully. They all chimed in that if anyone could do it, he could. They started talking about what it could possibly be that held the fabric of time together. They all knew if they could figure something to try, they'd be able to fabricate it for sure. That was a very good question and they were all racking their brains to figure out a suggestion.

Finally Steven spoke up. "Ok if time is space distorted by energy; then is it the space we're looking for or the energy? Is it the byproduct of the two combined to create time?" no one answered as it was rhetorical and just something for them to chew on as he continued.

"Or the other theory that space time is made of one of three things: graviton particles, cosmic strings and quantum foam. Now if these are what makes up time, we can distinguish graviton particles and pull them from the space enclosing them. They are minute particles surrounding everything and cannot be seen or felt without specific equipment. Think about dust in the sunshine coming through a window. It's always there, but you can't see it because the right circumstance doesn't exist—the light being missing. Cosmic strings are unseen as well yet seem to be the pull against gravity and the means by which the graviton particles travel through space and time. As far as quantum foam, could it be the by-product of the first two and that's the part that we're seeing as ooze and is spilling forth from the tear like water from a broken pipe?" They'd have to think on all that a bit.

Steven went on to say that if energy is the fabric where each particle moving around has an energy distribution and the total energy at any point in space is determined by the amount of particles in that specific space, then the total energy density would be thicker or thinner depending on the amount of particles present. Therefore if they could move the particles or redistribute them to the area where there are fewer particles, then the fabric would be thicker, sealed and stronger. At least theoretically that would work. Now to determine how to introduce particles into the thin or gaping area to strengthen or patch, if you will, the hole or thin spot. Also what kind of particles would they need to use and how would they place or inject them where they needed to be to repair the rift?

Definitely if this could be figured out and accomplished, then they knew for sure to stagger their launch sites to many various places to avoid rifts in the future. It also could mean that the particles were already moving around like cells in a human body to repair itself, but the constant reopening of the rift is like tearing the scab off repeatedly before the wound could heal.

So their theory that the time cells were falling out seemed more likely than ever and they needed to find a way to replicate the cells or cause them to multiply on their own, like blood clotting to stop the patient from bleeding to death.

Chapter 20

Everyone was up again when the chopper came. They had been deep in thought when they retired early the night before. Thinking. Thinking about time, space, the rift, and particles. They were feeling a little defeated and knew they needed rest and a fresh look at what was happening in order to start formulating new ways to think about the problem.

Breakfast was uneventful and quiet as still everyone was in deep thought. They were just going through the motions. The same routine they'd been in for weeks could almost take care of itself without much concentration from the team. So without having to consider what they were really doing, they were using the power of their minds to rethink and mull over what had happened, what was tried and what might be considered a plausible act to try next.

Ryan was the first to speak. "So if we need particles to fill the gap, do the particles have to be exactly like what came out of the gap or can we patch the hole with a new substance? We putty walls with holes in them, paint over and they look fine. Can we do this with the rift? Can the fabric of time be repaired using other particles, or will it cause a duct tape effect? I guess I'm saying could it become an eyesore on the atmosphere, or maybe show through to the naked eye when we walk past it? Is there a danger that we would cause a big bulky plug in the hole, or do we expect the universe to just accept what we shoot it up with and distribute it where it's needed to heal itself? I'm wondering if we use coal dust, for example, to fill the hole, will it be just a lump of coal hanging in the air for all to see and have no idea how to fix that new anomaly, or do we have to find a particle that is either so small it's nearly invisible, or once encapsulated in the atmosphere, will it become invisible to the naked eye? Then there's the problem of introducing it into the rift. I think we should blast it into the opening before it closes, so the bulk of the particles are contained right there where we need them, but if we send too many at once, we may just blast them into the future instead of into the tear. If we can send several layers of particles in, then they can adhere to what's there and start building up the fabric, like dirt stuck to the kitchen rug. If you shake it, it flies off, but just lying there, it's not noticeable at all. I also think the particles have to be like crushed sand. Very small and then reduced again to a powder-like substance that will adhere to the atmosphere inside the rift, like dust does on our furniture at home. I'm thinking we can use a fan to scatter the dust particles into the rift. That would make them light and airy, as anything heavy will just drop to the ground before it ever enters inside. It can't be too strong or it will blow through like another passenger traveling. What do you all think?"

They thought it made sense, every bit of it; and every question he posed made sense as well, but no one had any answers. It seemed like it would work, but so did going back in time to stop the experiment.

Margaret finally spoke up. "I've been mulling this over since it happened and I've been listening to everyone's comments and thoughts on what was going on, things to try and how to fix it. Everything we've tried has failed, but I think I've come to a conclusion about it all. It seems to me from what we've discovered already that opening the rift did not cause the tear since Alan stopped the experiment we did yesterday from ever happening, so it couldn't have caused the problem. With that being said, we now know the rift was caused by wear and tear in the same spot or some other anomaly causing it to be thin enough to split on its own. I am going to propose that having dealt with sound waves before, this rift was caused by a weakened spot in the fabric along with a sudden energy boost from the lightning, and an echo effect from the thunder. I believe these beautiful West Virginia mountains are positioned precisely in the spot needed to cause the echo and that's why it's opening repeatedly. Every time the echo bounces back, it will reopen because the power source is still there. Lightning's power can be physically measured in the air and the ground for quite a while after a strike and we had many strikes, close together during that storm. I know it sounds far-fetched, but we had everything we needed for this natural phenomena to have occurred. That storm was horrendous. The lightning and thunder were severe and could easily cause enough power and echo to cause this rift to keep opening. It was basically the same combination we have been using with the plutonium and the tachyon pulse. The echo is doing the exact same thing as the pulse does for our power source. From accounts in the Bermuda Triangle and other areas at sea, almost everyone was involved in a storm of similar magnitude just before planes disappeared or ships were lost. I believe they were transported back in time or into the future. Quite possibly in the exact location they were when it happened and if that's so, they would never surface to be found. They would be buried at sea. I also believe if we find this to be true to the best of our beliefs, then there is nothing that we can do to fix it. We will have to wait until the echo stops on its own, and it will. The bounce time should be starting to lengthen between hits. The echo cannot effectively stay in motion between these mountains. Everything in between the mountains where it's bouncing will cause it to slow to a stop. Just our passing through here daily will absorb some of the sound waves and slow the bounce effect. I project within the next couple hours, we'll find the time between openings will increase substantially until it totally stops on its own; OR, the power from the lightning will eventually be used up and there won't be enough to keep reopening the rift. Theoretically, it should also weaken with every opening of the rift. We may never know if it's the power, the echo or both that are causing the problematic reopening rift, but I do believe given time it will fix itself. If you'll recall, we are not using a stopwatch to determine exact timing either, we're just looking at our watches and stating it's almost time. I purpose, since we're all here watching to make sure nothing goes through, that we stop recording and check the exact time on the recording to see if there's been any change since the beginning. This will tell us if I'm on the right track."

Wow, that stunned them all, but Alan was the first one to speak. "OK, let's definitely check the tape and if you're correct, then do we try to absorb more of the sound waves' echo or the power to help slow this thing down? We can't let it keep bouncing around, someone's going to notice and all our plans will be ruined along with, quite possibly, the whole world. You see if the government gets this technology and something like this happens, they will try to cover it up instead of understanding and fixing it if possible. We know when it's going to happen, we can make sure we're close to the rift when the power or echo comes back and our bodies can help absorb some of the energy or sound waves, plus we can bring our tents, pillows and clothes into this area. Every bit of fabric will absorb a little. It may still take a while to stop it all, but we've got to do something to help expedite the plan. Margaret, you and Denver have been working with power sources, is there a machine we can build or have on hand already that can absorb some of the energy? We know where it's going, so we can position the container there at the mouth of the rift to capture as much as possible each time it opens."

"We certainly do have a way; and it's pretty simple too." Denver was quick to answer. "We build a capacitor. Actually we need to build two of them, one for each Chevy. We'll charge them with the power we absorb from the lightning and they'll be a back-up power unit for our time travels. We've got plenty of wire and metal, so it will be easy to build the conductors and insulators it will require to complete the capacitors. Could it really be this easy to stop and close the rift? We've pounded our brains and how simple an idea. I sure hope it works. It will take a load off all our minds."

"Agreed!" was chimed in by everyone in the group. "Let's get busy, who wants to help me?" Denver asked.

Denver, Alison, and George decided they would build them. Margaret went to check the recordings to see if the timing had changed on the appearances of the rift. Alison had never built a capacitor, so she wanted to learn. She felt like she might need to know if anything went wrong while time traveling. They gladly accepted her help and were happy to teach her. "So it's like a battery?" she asked. "It's actually a device used to store an electric charge, so it's sort of like a battery. It has one or more pairs of conductors separated by an insulator. So you don't just pop it into a compartment where an old battery had been, but it would have to be wired into the machine you want to power with it. Basic principal is the same since it's a power cell, just hardwired differently." Denver explained. Alison fully understood what he meant and continued to do what he told her to get her's built before George got his built. It wasn't really a race, just some friendly competition to help make the task more enjoyable. She and Denver actually finished first. She was slower at it as she was learning, but Denver's extra hands prepping the second conductor after helping her do the first one, while she installed everything into the insulator helped them gain the advantage. It only took about thirty minutes to gather the supplies and make them as they were pretty easy to do, so they were ready for the next rift.

Margaret had determined that the rifts were gaining about fifteen seconds between openings over where they started from in the beginning. The capacitors would slow this dramatically over the next couple openings. They positioned their equipment right in front of the rift and anchored them heavily so they wouldn't be sucked into it.

Then they backed away and let the capacitors absorb as much energy as possible. They all stood between the path the energy should be taking to open the rift so they absorbed some energy as well. Alison's hair stood straight up from the static energy she absorbed. It was like touching one of those static electricity bulbs at the science fair when they were kids. At least they knew it was working. There were cheers and several fist bumps and high fives being passed around. They'd found and were fixing the problem! Now to reset the equipment and wait for the next rift to open. They were ready at the twenty minute mark, but were amazed, it took thirty minutes for the next one. That meant they'd drained quite a bit of energy from the bounce. They figured a few more times and it wouldn't have enough energy left to open the rift and they would definitely not reopen from that spot again, even though they didn't really think that would matter. Always cautious.

After a few more openings, they decided a couple of them would stay and man the equipment while the rest headed back to the camp to start dinner and their chores. It would soon be nightfall and they'd work in shifts to finish gathering as much power as they could, to stop the rift.

Those staying brought their chairs together so they could talk while they waited for the surge to reappear. Margaret worked on erasing all the footage of the rift opening on its own and then headed for camp to help get everything done. There, it was the same as every other day. Showers, cooking, gathering firewood and water, laundry to be gathered for the next day's washing and securing the stuff they brought back from the clearing. They hadn't brought the capacitors back to the camp as they wanted to retrieve some more energy from the echo. Hopefully they could have it stopped during the night and take them to the future then. Tom wanted to be sure they took them to the future before wake-up call in the morning. Even if the rift was still opening, he didn't want anything out of order. He'd already set his alarm to get him up early enough to have the people back from the clearing long before their six o'clock wake up call. He'd take them to the future himself.

When dinner was ready, they ate and then George and Alan switched places with Steven and Ryan, who'd stayed at the clearing, so they could eat and get ready for bed. George and Alan manned the capacitors through the night. The last opening was at four o'clock and it was three hours since the one before. They were thinking maybe it was enough to stop it, but time would tell. Tom was there at five and he did the honors of time travel with the capacitors. After he'd tucked them in the storage unit, he didn't linger but returned to camp to make sure things were ok before he woke the others.
He and George returned to camp with the gear from the clearing and Alan stayed deep in the tree line to watch for the rift to reappear.

Tom talked to the man in the chopper and gave him their food order for the next day. They were nearly out of a couple essentials, like milk. Then he made sure no one slept through the noise of the chopper and they began their morning regimen.

Chapter 21

Margaret was cooking pancakes, bacon, sausage, and French toast. She even whipped up a fresh strawberry sauce for the French toast. It was looking amazing and smelling good too. They were all feeling pretty good since they'd figured out what was going on with the rift and had been able to stop it happening. George had filled them in on the progress with absorbing the power through the night and how long it had been since an opening occurred. They were sure it was over. Everyone toasted Margaret when he told them about it and congratulated her on being the one to figure it out. She was very modest about it and told them any of them would have figured it out soon too; it was just a matter of looking at everything from every angle.

As soon as they'd eaten, Tom went to relieve Alan so he could come have breakfast and hit the sack for some rest as he and George had been up most of the night, and they needed to sleep at least four hours before joining the group for their light lunch. Denver was making sandwiches and packing fruit for their lunch today. He had finished his chores and decided he'd like sandwiches so he figured if it was his choice, he'd need to be the cook. It was just sandwiches after all and he could cook if he wanted to. His mother made sure of that when he was growing up. He mostly liked to make spaghetti and meatballs. He decided he'd like to do that for dinner, huh, he seemed in the mood to cook all of a sudden, or maybe his stomach thought the idea of spaghetti was a good one. Anyway he spoke up and told them all he'd be cooking if they had the needed supplies and also informed the ladies, he'd still get the water for the day. Alison informed him they did have the necessary ingredients and since he was still doing the heavy work, she'd make the salads and toast to go with the spaghetti. Steven spoke up and said he could do fried apple pies if anyone wanted those. All hands went up and they all laughed. Everyone's mouths were watering already and they had just finished breakfast.

Myra said she thought she'd talk to Tom about a reprieve this afternoon. It had been a few days since they'd had much free time, so she was going to suggest a hike or maybe some swimming in the deep place in the creek. Just something to relieve the stress they'd been under with the rift and give them some muscle stretching time. Their bodies needed to move. They all agreed with that and thought that was a great plan.

It didn't take much longer before all the camp was cleaned and straightened up. Steven and Ryan headed to the creek to do laundry and would join the rest of them soon in the clearing. It was a beautiful day for Myra's proposed outing and they were all looking forward to seeing if Tom had any objections. He didn't and they were getting excited to play a while. He wanted to get everything set up for the next time travel before they left. They moved everything around and decided they would do twenty feet moves around the center until they'd completed the circle and then they'd move the machine's center spot to another location so as not to cause any more thin spots in the fabric of time; just in case. Once they'd moved all the equipment and secured it all, they headed back to camp via a different route so as to have one hike under their belt for the day and to enjoy the beauty of the mountains in West Virginia before their time was finished there. Just as they were starting to leave, Steven and Ryan joined them. They'd finished the laundry in record time and were thankful they'd gotten there before the others left. Everything was lush and in full bloom. The state flower, the Rhododendron, was blooming and its scent was magnificent. The flowers were huge and were so pretty to look at. The forest smelled so clean and fresh. There was only the sound of nature, no traffic or sirens, just birds singing and squirrels chattering as they scurried along looking for nuts. It was cooler, due to the thick vegetation, but it was still very comfortable during the day. At night it got a little cool, but that's what made the fire so nice. They were winding their way down the mountain to the stream. They'd noticed a couple nice spots where the water looked deep enough to swim. They hadn't bothered with suits, they would just play I their shirts and shorts. Denver and Jody were carrying their lunch and by the time they reached the bottom, they'd probably be ready to eat. Then hike on down to the big swimming hole they'd seen on their first day there, while doing recognizance. It should be just a long enough hike to settle their lunch. Things just seemed to go right in nature and this place was magical. No wonder they called it "Almost Heaven".

The most eventful thing they saw was a doe and her twin fawns across the creek. They were pretty far away, but they still bolted and ran a few hundred feet away before stopping to look back. When they saw they weren't being followed, they continued to graze in the tall grass that grew at the edge of the trees. When scared again, they leaped toward the trees and disappeared into the darkness.

They all loved the wildlife and the beauty that surrounded them was sort of surreal.

They played, splashed and swam for a couple hours before the last one was lying on the creek bank basking in the sunshine and absorbing the ray's warmth as it kissed their skin.

None of them wanted to go back to the camp, but it would be almost a two hour hike back and all up hill, so they'd be tired and hungry once they arrived and they weren't having a real quick meal. The spaghetti and trimmings would take nearly an hour and a half to prepare. If they wanted it to be really good, it had to simmer a bit. It had been such a nice afternoon, just relaxing and enjoying each other's company. They'd worked their muscles for sure and would probably feel it the next morning, but they were all in good shape, so they wouldn't be too sore, just a little because they hadn't had a lot of exercise since they'd gotten there.

They groaned at the thought of having to leave, but got up, brushed themselves off and headed for the camp. "Where do you want to travel to, if we ever manage to get this time travelling thing going?" Myra asked. "Personally, I want to go to Egypt during the time of Cleopatra." They all stopped, looked at her (she winked at them-so they'd know she was just being cautious) and began telling her where they'd like to go.

Denver "I want to go to the moon for the first moon landing. Wait that brings up another question, if we manage to do time travel, do you think we'll be confined to Earth?" They all pondered that for a few minutes and decided if they ever got to travel, they'd have to experiment with that one. It would be hard to get a GPS reading on another planet or the moon. Tom said he was pretty sure they'd be confined to this planet, but no confines on when on this planet at all.

Margaret "I want to go to Greece, and specifically the island of Rhodes, during the time the Colossus statue was being finished. I think in its original glory, it would have been amazing."

Alan "I'd like to meet Einstein, anywhere he happened to be."

George "I'd like to go to Rome for the first Olympic games. I'd love to watch the gladiators fight."

Alison "I'd like to meet Mother Theresa and the Dalai Lama; two of the greatest humanitarians ever."

Steven "I want to go to Jerusalem at the time of the crucifixion of Christ. I think that would answer every question I ever had about Christianity."

Ryan "I want to witness the birth of Hawaii. That volcano erupting must have been magnificent. It would be something to witness Earth giving life. Spewing forth from under the ocean, rising above the surface to create an island. Can you imagine the fireworks from that!"

Jody "I think I'd like to have been there when Kennedy was assassinated, I'd know exactly where to be to know for sure who did it and if they were acting alone. I'd like to debunk every conspiracy theory out there." Not that I could tell the world, but I would know and that's all that mattered really.

"Wow that's some pretty diverse places we all want

to explore." Tom exclaimed. "I myself would like to go into the future a thousand years and see how this world has progressed. If I had to go into the past, however, I'd like to meet Abraham Lincoln. He was a man ahead of his time."

They all mused about those and other places all the way back to the camp. Then it was busy time to get dinner ready, showers, and chores done for the next day.

Denver and Alison immediately washed their hands and started dinner.

Steven headed for the shower first, then came back and immediately started on the fried apple pies. As each one was finished, he put it in the iron skillet on a warm burner to keep them hot for dessert.

They talked some more through dinner about places they'd like to travel. Places they've been already and special events they were witness to in person. Tom and Myra had more of those to talk about than the young folks, but they were fascinated by their stories, nonetheless.

Soon it was time for bed and they started cleaning up the dishes and camp area. Then they began gathering the stuff they'd need for the morning. When all that was complete, they got ready for bed and said their good-nights.

It was about two in the morning when they were all awakened by the extremely loud noise of the camp stove being turned over. Everyone leaped from their tents bearing makeshift weapons, lights, and air horns. The noise itself should have scared off a bear, but they weren't taking chances.

There near the camp stove, caught in the bright lights was a man carrying a backpack.

"Wait, don't shoot me or anything! I'm with NASA. I was hiking in to check on you guys and see how things were coming when I got lost and made a couple wrong turns. I've been wondering around looking for your camp. I lost my flashlight in the stream and couldn't see very well as there's no moon out tonight and your camp is in this small area inside all this magnificent forest. With all the dense trees and underbrush, I just couldn't see where I was going. I'm sorry to have awakened you all, I was hoping to just slip in and put my sleeping bag near the fire and then talk to everyone in the morning since I didn't get here on time last night."

Tom was the first to speak, but no one had lowered their weapons yet. "What's your name?" Ethen Miller was his reply. "Show me your ID and I mean your NASA ID." He did produce his NASA ID and it matched his name and picture. Tom pulled out his NASA ID and the look was the same. If it was a fake, it was a good one. "You won't mind if we search your backpack and your person for any weapons then." He immediately handed over his pack and then spread his legs and arms for a search. The only thing they found was a Swiss army knife, which they kept until they could get verification on his real identity. "Why didn't you just make camp and walk on in here in the morning?" He admitted to not being accustomed to the outdoors and didn't really know how to start a fire. "Why didn't you have NASA bring you in?" "I'm afraid of helicopters and flying in general really." He began "So I told them I'd drive to the area and then hike it. I would have been here before dark had I not gotten lost. This really is a wilderness, but it's a beautiful place too. There are so many different kinds of trees and flowers, the scent is amazing. I was really enjoying the hike until I realized I was lost and wouldn't make your camp before dark; then I started to panic a little. I mean I know there are bears around and I wouldn't have a fire or anything, so I kept going. I figured I'd walk till I found you or fell over from exhaustion." He finished.

Well he looked like a scientist and they had been expecting someone, but they were still going to be wary until he was checked out in the morning.

Denver spoke up and said he'd take the watch, there was less than four hours left before the start of their day anyway and everyone could go back to sleep. Mr. Miller could have his place in the tent to get some rest. They agreed and headed back to bed. Denver didn't trust him and was going to be extra careful checking him out and making sure he didn't do anything out of the ordinary. He grabbed his jacket and shoes then put some coffee on so he'd stay awake, stoked the fire and took his book out with him to read.

When the chopper came Tom asked them about sending someone. They said they had and gave a full description of him along with his name. They apologized for the scare and not letting them know ahead of time he was coming. That was an internal slip-up. He would be extracted in two weeks via helicopter so he wouldn't get lost again going back. They informed him that Mr. Miller was well versed in Tom's calculations and theories on time travel and was there to watch them travel or help them figure out why it wasn't working. They were to give him everything he asked for and make any adjustments he requested so every possible effort could be made to achieve their goal. He'd be there for two weeks and if they were no closer to the goal, then the project would be shut down. Tom exploded, "You promised me four months to work out any issues we had, we've been working diligently and just haven't been able to get the exact power level to make it work. I want my full time allotted." The answer was "Sorry, orders from headquarters."

At the beginning of the conversation, Tom thought that it was strange he could go back by helicopter when he was so afraid of them, but he also knew this guy was there to spy on them. Now he knew for a fact that this guy was going to force them into performing everything he could in those two weeks. Well they'd give him a great show, several of them, actually. Tom ordered more squirrels as he was sure they'd destroy every one they had today if not tomorrow. They were serious and they were taking over.

Everyone was up and starting their chores, breakfast was on. Denver had started cooking since he was up anyway. He made omelets and toast. He was nearly finished when he asked Mr. Miller how he liked his. Once he had the requested ingredients, he made one to order for Mr. Miller and then made his own as well.

They all knew why he was there, but no one was saying much. They were oohing and ahhhing over the omelets and thinking about everything around the clearing. It was all clear, safe and set up just like they wanted it to be. They were also thinking that they were so glad he hadn't showed up two days earlier in the midst of the echo effect on the rift. They were well versed on their codes and knew that not one of them would make a slip because in their minds, they'd trained themselves to acknowledge that they truly hadn't been able to complete time travel.

Margaret was especially glad she'd made them talk about not achieving time travel yet on their hike back. If he were near, and she believed he had probably been observing them at that time, then he'd know for sure; due to their casual conversation, that they were still searching for the elusive combination to make it work.

Once breakfast was over, they all began gathering their stuff to take to the clearing. Margaret picked up a fresh bag of nuts for the squirrels as she knew they'd be blowing up several of them that day and she felt they at least needed a banquet for their last meal.

Mr. Miller was just observing everyone and they'd done this all so many times, so they were acting very normal as it all came naturally. They'd developed a nice routine for their daily activities.

When they got to the clearing, Tom explained that NASA was pulling the plug if they couldn't achieve success by the end of the two weeks when Mr. Miller would be leaving. Several of them were starting to complain that they'd been doing all they could. This stuff took time. Men had been working on this for centuries and they were all confident in Tom's theories, even NASA had studied it and agreed. Now they just needed to find the right power source and level of power. "They know all that, I'm just sorry we haven't found that. We've tried every source we have available so NASA has sent Mr. Miller to try whatever he thinks we need to do. We all want this to happen, so accept him as part of the team and be as cooperative with him as you've been with me and maybe, just maybe, we'll find it before they shut us down." Tom played his part well and they all knew his hidden meaning.

Altogether, they started agreeing and making comments that they'd just felt inferior or that NASA thought they weren't trying; but Tom was right and he was just the newest member of the team.

They separated and started setting up the experiment. They were going to try various amounts of gamma power, starting with low rays and increasing to full capacity until something opened or it blew up the squirrel. They knew what would happen, they'd done it before. They knew this was not going to work, but they were amazing actors, they showed much anticipation and hope, like it had been their first time doing it. Mr. Miller checked and double checked all the settings before they began. When he seemed satisfied, he gave the go-ahead. It was just a few seconds before the squirrel was cooked.

They jumped in, cleaned up the debris, moved fifteen feet to the right and started setting it up again. Mr. Miller was curious as to the move. It's just to keep us out of the squirrel blood and guts. We do run a pretty tidy ship Tom told him; and these things do carry rabies, so we can't be too careful. It only takes a few minutes to move and readjust stuff. Mr. Miller nodded and they proceeded. "I'm just trying to understand." He smiled.

They gave the gamma rays four attempts before moving on to the next power source. Magnetic. They were all secretly waiting for the squirrel in the box to disappear and actually be stuck to the magnet. Mr. Miller was just as surprised as they were when it happened the first time. "Sorry." Tom apologized. "But we've tried all this and it hasn't worked, so we didn't tell you in case you found something we missed. We've tried every power source here and nothing works. Do you think atmosphere would make a difference? Too much or not enough humidity? I've racked my brain trying to find another element that could be the problem, but nothing works. Do you think the cage we have the squirrel in would make a difference? Do you think we should just send an empty cage, maybe the squirrel is the problem? I don't think any of this is an issue, but something has to be. We're using enough power to blow up buildings, so the amount of power shouldn't be the problem, unless the fabric is so strong that it requires super power to penetrate it; and if that's the case, we'll never achieve time travel as that much power is not sustainable. I don't know why it's not working, but I wanted to throw a few things out there for you to mull over. Maybe your fresh look at things will uncover something. Anything is worth a try. We just want to do this so badly and we were and still are all convinced it will work. Sorry, I've rambled on so long, but I thought maybe you could find the issue. I just REALLY want this."

Mr. Miller assured him that they'd been doing everything right, and that something had to be missing. That's why he was there, just to double check all the calculations, formulas and the way the tests were being set up. He wanted to test every method of power at least four times with four different power levels.

They all agreed and would comply with everything he requested. After a long day and twelve less squirrels, they called it finished. Hoping tomorrow would be a better day.

They secured the equipment and headed back to camp.

Mr. Miller offered to cook for them. He said he made an amazing meatloaf that worked well when you didn't have an oven. He made it into patties and fried it on the camp stove. He would make au gratin potatoes and fried cabbage to go with it. They thought that sounded yummy, so they showed him to the stove and secured the ingredients he requested. Alison asked if they wanted blueberry cobbler for dessert. Everyone chimed in a great big YES! Mr. Miller asked how she would prepare it without an oven. "Oh we have an oven of sorts." She explained and showed him the log where she was preparing kindling to start her fire. Between working on his menu, he watched carefully how she made the standing log into an oven with fire inside and a covered iron skillet on top. He was very impressed and said "of all the times I've been camping, I've never seen" he stopped. "You've never seen what Mr. Miller, or whatever your name is? You've been camping a lot and are not the bumbling idiot about the woods as you claimed. We know you're working for NASA to help finish this and then steal it or shut us down early if you see it's not going to work. We are called geniuses for a reason you know." Alison accused.

"You're absolutely correct on all counts. I am Samuel Perkins, a theoretical physicist and professor of mathematical physics. I was brought in to look at your work and I agree all calculations are correct and the only issue is the powering of it all." Alison gasped. "I've heard of you and I've read a couple of your papers. It's an honor to work with you sir. I hope you can solve the problem because we've done everything we know to do and have failed. "I hope so too in a way." He said. "What do you mean professor?" "Just that I'm not sure the government will do the right thing with it if they get their hands on it. I almost hope we fail. It could be bad for the world if they start playing with "fixing' things too much." "Wow professor, I hadn't thought about that. You raise a good point." She told him. "But there is nothing we can do about it if we do find the key."

Everyone in camp was listening intently to their conversation. They all knew that he may be telling the truth and he may be trying to gain their confidence so they'd spill the beans. They were all on the same page, they hadn't discovered it yet; just like planned and rehearsed! They couldn't trust him no matter how much they wanted to. It was too dangerous for them and their world.

Tom spoke up just then and said he had a severe headache. It had been coming on since yesterday, so he was going to retire as soon as he'd eaten and see if he could sleep it off. Everyone looked at him knowingly and many said they hoped it went away quickly and if he needed anything to call out and they'd get it for him. Myra said she'd get him some aspirin now and an ice pack for his head when he retired for the evening. She immediately went to the medical tent and brought back a couple pills for him. He took them and pressed his hands against his temples.

When dinner was ready, they all made their plates and sat down to eat. The meatloaf was very good as was the au gratin potatoes and the fried cabbage. It was a good combination too. But the best part of the whole day was the blueberry cobbler Alison had made. It was superb and even Mr. Perkins was impressed.

As stated as soon as he'd eaten, Tom got up and said his good-nights. Myra followed him to get his ice pack fixed. Tom wrote and told her that he knew Mr. Perkins could not be trusted. He was too quick to see if they'd get on board with not wanting the government to have it. He also told her they needed to make sure each team member knew this and to be extra careful as he thought he was probably bugging the place when he tripped over the stove and was found out. She indicated she'd tell the girls once they were in their tents and they could each work their way through telling the guys.

They talked a while after dinner and then did their chores for the morning and headed off to bed. The tents began to glow with their computers, tablets, or phones since they had internet and wanted to connect with family and friends quickly before going to sleep. Nearly all of them texted or messaged family members "No luck yet" like they did most nights. Keeping up the farce!

Mr. Perkins connected with the project manager at NASA. He typed his messages instead of snapchat, skype or any other method he could have used to communicate with them. He updated them on their progress and had attempted to make friends or at least help them to believe he was on their side. He told NASA that he felt they were genuinely trying as hard as they could to make this project succeed. They sounded perplexed as to why things were not working and threw out many scenarios they thought he might be able to help them with or shed light on as to any issue that may be interfering with their tests. The calculations were correct and he'd let them set up each test, then he would double check it. He too was perplexed as to why nothing was working. Progress would continue until all aspects and every method was explored in the shortest time possible. He told them if Tom hadn't ordered more squirrels and nuts, then they'd probably better bring a few more in the morning. He told them there was much comradery among them all and they truly were working together to accomplish the goal. They all spoke of things they'd like to see and places they'd like to go and were surprised when he'd mentioned that they might not want the government to have this in its repertoire of weapons. It was like it had never occurred to them and for that he was glad and thought NASA should be as well. He'd keep them informed and keep the projects moving as quickly as he could to further the progress. He again told them that he believed Tom's calculations were right and if his didn't work, than it was probably a very lost cause.

Chapter 22

Morning came and so did the helicopter with more squirrels, they'd killed twelve the day before and would probably do the same today. Nothing else was needed for the camp except some coffee and milk. Nuclear, laser and Plutonium were on the agenda for today. If they didn't succeed with those, they would have to try whatever else Mr. Perkins came up with. If he had no suggestions that ended up working within the two week period, then their shot at history would be over, at least until they could find another backer to let them further their research. Tom wasn't a spring chicken any longer and he figured this would be his last chance at fame, but fame was no longer what he wanted—he just needed to talk it up that way. He wanted to be free of NASA and any other government agency so he could travel through time and see things he never could have, experience great events in history first hand and live a thrilling life for the rest of his days, not stuck in a lab or calculating equations and developing theories, as much as he liked those things, but really living!

Everyone got busy with their respective chores, showers, breakfast, and it was laundry day for Alan and Myra. Breakfast was biscuits, gravy, fried potatoes, tomatoes, bacon and sausage. A true West Virginia breakfast; hearty and stick to your ribs food. It was delicious too. Once everyone was ready to head out, Myra and Alan headed over the hill towards the stream with the laundry, while the rest of them headed to the clearing for experiments. Myra and Alan were going to fix lunch when they got back from doing the laundry and had it all hanging to dry. They'd decided on cheese, crackers, grapes, bagel bites and cream cheese. They still had steaks in the coolers so they'd be eating pretty heartily that night as well. No need to send them back with NASA at the end of the two weeks; or sooner, if they decided to pull the plug earlier. They could enjoy them just fine right there, grilled on the open fire. She made sure she told Alan in four words the secret message she needed him to know for sure. Don't trust possible bugs. She whispered in his ear while they were at the stream doing laundry so the water would camouflage the sounds. He was already thinking the same thing.

Tom and the team were not long setting up the first experiment. Mr. Perkins went over it all with a fine-toothed comb. He found every setting and coordinate to be exactly what it needed to be. So the countdown was on. Everyone was in position and Tom engaged the nuclear power. The cross power grid lit up and then the energy was fed to the center machine to cause a distortion, but nothing happened. It didn't slice through or create an opening for the squirrel to pass through. It was as though they had no power at all. At least the squirrel was safe—this time anyway. They tried different power levels and each time nothing happened at all. Mr. Perkins said it was plain to see that nuclear power was definitely not the means to open a portal in time in which someone could pass from one place to another.

"So you don't want to do more experiments with the nuclear then? Moving it closer or farther away?" Tom asked. Mr. Perkins saw no need.

Next they were trying the laser. It was the easiest of all mediums to work with. It could be controlled and directed faster and easier than any other source. It was definitely powerful enough, it would just depend on if it was the right power. It seemed some power or energy was just absorbed into space instead of separating it. A laser beam set high enough should drill right through anything in front of it. Three times, they increased the power and directed it to slightly different spots, but they had no success. Just like the first time they did laser testing, before Mr. Perkins got there, nothing happened. Mr. Perkins decided on one more try and the power would be greater than before. Tom told him they'd set it up after lunch. His stomach had just growled. After his headache had subsided, he'd gotten very hungry.

Myra and Alan hadn't been there very long before they pulled out the snacks they'd prepared and everyone sat down to relax a bit. They were always tense when doing experiments because with the power levels they were working with, anything could go wrong. They only took a half hour to enjoy their snacks and were stretching muscles as they got up to return to their tasks.

Once they got everything set up. Mr. Perkins decided one of the aiming mirrors needed to be moved slightly. When they pulled the trigger to release the laser, it was off target and shot into the sky slicing off the tops of about six trees and traveling about thirty miles towards a very large mountain. Fortunately it only made a hole into the mountaintop about ten feet deep and twenty feet in diameter. The team went ballistic. "We've not damaged anything but squirrels the whole time we've been here and in less than two days, you've damaged a mountain! Well the National Enquirer will be showing up soon, looking for the aliens who attacked West Virginia. Man we had it right, why did you have to go messing with it? We went through every measure possible to keep it a secret that we were here and now this. Were you trying to end the experiments? Was this your plan all along? How could you make such an amateur mistake? First year students wouldn't have done that. They may as well extract us now because we'll be hunted down very soon and strung up if we're not careful. These people take pride in their state and its beautiful mountains, they're not going to stand idly by and let this slide. I can't believe it! I just can't believe it!" Those comments and more were coming from everyone.

"I truly am sorry, but NASA will be the ones coming to investigate and they'll cover it up with some plausible excuse. They'll have everyone believing their story before a day's over. No one will be looking here since that's thirty miles away." I'll contact them as soon as we get satellite service tonight. I'll explain it's all my fault and I'll take full responsibility for it.

"You sure will, MR. PERKINS!" Tom was still livid. "Don't you think anyone might have seen the beam coming from this direction? People around here can see the sky; they're not encased in tall buildings. Why, they even have people who sit on their porches a little every day just to watch the clouds go by. I'm telling you, someone will be snooping around and it won't be anyone official, it will be someone who lives around here and maybe hunts in these woods and knows their way around.

Next won't be stories about the aliens, it will be about secret government experiments!"

"Maybe we're all too worked up to do any more experiments today. Let's take a break and have some fun. I saw a guitar in the tent; maybe we could have some singing and fun around the campfire and start fresh tomorrow after we've all calmed down." Mr. Perkins began. "Maybe you can go have some fun and we'll get back to what we were doing before you came." Tom said rather loudly. That's when Myra stepped in and suggested a good long hike might do them all good. They'd been cooped up a bit and the exercise would be good for them all. She smiled at Tom and he relented. "I want you in the middle of the group so we can keep an eye on you Mr. Perkins. Don't want you destroying any more things in this beautiful state. I'm telling you everyone here has a gun and if it were my home state and someone was tearing it up, I myself might just be tempted to shoot them and leave them where they wouldn't be found." Tom glared at him. "Why don't you call me Sam." He suggested. Tom glared at him again and said "I'll stick to Mr. Perkins if that's alright with you, I generally use first names for my friends." Myra sent a charming smile in Mr. Perkins direction and he relented to silence. Denver announced he'd lead the pack.

They secured all the equipment and made sure nothing was left on and all locks were in place. They definitely didn't want someone stumbling in and taking the top off another mountain especially since they expected people to be snooping now. Then they headed down the mountain for their hike. Myra had never seen Tom mad, but he was about to explode on Mr. Perkins. She had to keep the atmosphere light or this was going to be an unbearable rest of the two weeks.

Denver was pointing out trees, bushes and flowers along the way and telling everyone the names of each. Margaret picked a rhododendron blossom and kept smelling it as they walked. She asked if any of them had ever worked with scents and oils. She'd like to make some cologne out of these, or air freshener that really smelled like the flowers and not some chemical interpretation. Ryan said he'd google it when the internet came up that night and they could try to make some. She was delighted and said she'd gather some on the way back so they'd be fresher and she wouldn't have to carry them the whole way.

Once the tension was over and everyone calmed down with the quietness of the forest, it was really an enjoyable trip. Birds were singing and the beavers were working at the creek. They saw six deer in a clearing. The deer just watched them walk by as they kept eating the tall grass. They saw a rabbit, two chipmunks chasing each other, a couple squirrels and some geese flew over. Everyone was smiling by the time they'd hiked an hour. Denver suggested they get a drink from the stream and refill their water canteens as most were almost empty. They might even sit a bit, take their shoes off and cool their feet in the stream. Jody told them if they had any kind of pin, he'd catch trout for dinner. He just needed something to hook in their mouths. Everyone thought that sounded better than the steaks they'd planned. They could always have those the next night. Tom had a pen, so Jody ran some string from his hooded shirt through the pen casing and hooked it to a long stick. The clip on the barrel would catch in the fish's lip long enough for him to pull it out if he was quick; and he was definitely quick. It was barely twenty minutes before he had a dozen on a string; that would be plenty for dinner, more than enough actually and maybe enough for two dinners. They could put half in the cooler for a couple days and then have fish again. He suggested Alison would probably have some fancy way of cooking it for the second meal. He'd grill it for tonight. She agreed she did and it was settled. She was a really good cook and they were glad they'd traded chores with her. She kept surprising them and they hadn't had the same dinner twice.

After the fishing, they all dried their feet and put their shoes back on for the hike back up the mountain. It was pretty steep in places, but they all looked out for one another. They'd managed to get the message to everyone about not trusting Mr. Perkins and to watch what they said at all times as there were potentially bugs placed in the camp, clearing, and surrounding areas.

It took them almost two hours to make the hike back up hill. They stopped for a couple ten minute breaks after each especially steep area. They saw a few more critters as well. They had no incidents, no sprains or falls, so it was definitely a good hike. Every time they really looked around, they appreciated this wilderness area more and more. They were all usually in the city somewhere and the solitude, peace and quiet of the forest was so refreshing. The sounds they did hear around them were calming noises. The chirp of the birds and the chatter of the squirrels and chipmunks was very enjoyable. Even the geese's honks as they flew overhead didn't interfere with the serene setting they were in. It was just so unlike the city that you couldn't help but relax. It calmed them and renewed their spirits. Maybe even start to forgive someone for the stupid mistake they'd made. Maybe that stupid mistake would draw tourists and be good for the economy in West Virginia. Tourism and coal were their major industries and coal had taken a big hit from environmental laws so they needed to boost tourism every way they could. Maybe some old man would invent something he saw in the sky about the time it happened and they'd have another mothman scenario going on in the state. There would be years of speculation on what or who caused that perfectly symmetrical cut out near the top of that mountain.

Once back at the camp, Denver and Jody took buckets of water about fifty feet away from camp and cleaned the fish, securing the cleanings in one bucket with a lid to be carried far from camp and emptied. No need inviting bears in. They brought the fish fillets back, sealed half in bags and put in the cooler before anything else. Ryan and George were cutting up vegetables to be grilled with the fish. Alan was fashioning a piece of fine wire into a grill pan so the fish could cook and not fall through the wire rack they were using over the fire. The vegetables would be in foil and Alison was going to make a sauce for them. Margaret decided to make some rice pilaf—it wouldn't take too long and Alison put bread dough in the iron skillet oven to bake. They'd have some nice hot rolls with their fish, rice and vegetables. Even Mr. Perkins helped, he put some coffee and tea on to brew. It was almost a five star restaurant out in those woods. It was fun too, with so many of them working together to make dinner. Myra realized they wouldn't have dessert so she whipped up a batch of peanut butter fudge and set it in the cooler to harden. They weren't paying attention as they were so busy and were very surprised when she produced it after dinner. What an excellent finish to an amazing dinner. They all congratulated each other and they decided they could do anything, they were the best team ever! "Well almost anything." Tom spoke up. "But then again I think with enough time and the right resources we could do that too. Sorry, I didn't mean to bring everyone down, I'm just a little bummed we're not accomplishing our goal. I'm going to remain positive though that with Mr. Perkins expertise, we'll get it done before we're made to quit."

"We'll do our best Tom." Mr. Perkins assured him. "Now can we have some of the guitar music I'm sure will set these hills on fire?" he asked.

Denver smiled and went to get his guitar. They sang a few of the songs they'd sung last time and laughed and talked about their hopes and dreams between songs. They all really did have bright futures in store. They would be sought after by the top companies and governments in the world for their knowledge. Plus they had a strong work ethic too and that was common knowledge as well. They were all on the verge of graduating and none really had any exact place they wanted to be and nothing else they wanted to study for now, so they were free birds awaiting where the headhunters would lead them and then make their decisions on what was offered them. They spent about an hour after dinner, just talking, singing, and enjoying themselves before they decided it was time to retire to their phones, laptops, and tablets to call home, do research and get ready for bed.

"Tom, I really am sorry about the mishap today. I didn't want to harm anything or anyone. I really am just here to help." Mr. Perkins apologized before heading to his tent. Since he'd taken Denver's place in the guy's tent that first night, Denver had made camp in the supply tent. He actually had more room there anyway.

Margaret and Ryan headed for the computer to research cologne and air fresheners to be made from the rhododendron blooms. It didn't take them long to determine that soaking them in oil would do the trick and later atomizers would allow that oil to become a fine mist for cologne. They wanted it to be fragrant, so they used more than the required amount of the blooms and it was smelling pretty good by the time they were ready to retire.

There wasn't a single one of them that wasn't asked about the mysterious "attack" on the mountain there in West Virginia, when they called home. They explained it was a rookie mistake by a not so rookie scientist. No one was harmed in their group or outside of it, but the mountain had a new cave.

They'd seen pictures of it on the news and were relieved when they'd spoken to their loved ones and knew they were unharmed.

Mike warned Tom to be extra careful of the people in the area and not to leave the camp unattended for fear the locals would definitely be snooping around. NASA had explained it as a satellite malfunction, which scared people more because if that's what happened, there could be more explosions all around the world. NASA had explained it was a rookie mistake and it wouldn't be happening again, but Mike suspected people would be looking around anyway. He'd seen a couple on the news pointing to where the beam had come from and it wasn't high in the sky.

Tom assured him that they'd have someone guard the camp while they were doing the experiments and appreciated him letting him know. He explained it would all be a circus if people found out what they were doing there.

Sam Perkins was true to his word. He told NASA about the incident, they already knew, they'd been contacted by the local government. He told them he'd made the mistake, but it didn't matter. They said they'd be there as usual every morning, but on the third morning, they'd all be leaving. That would give them two more days, after that it was over. They couldn't guarantee their safety after that. There were too many locals snooping around and it wouldn't be long until they started snooping in the direction of the camp.

Sam explained everything to them all that morning just before the helicopter arrived, so if they had any questions, they could radio then. The chopper pilot confirmed extraction to be in two days.

"Let's get to it then Mr. Perkins." Tom spoke up, breaking the silence that had fallen over the camp when the helicopter departed.

"Chores and breakfast as usual team, we've got experiments to perform. Our time has been cut way short and there are still squirrels to fry." He finished. "NOT funny." Myra said as she walked toward the cooler to get supplies to start breakfast.

They were all in sort of a sour mood. They weren't ready to call it quits, but mainly because they didn't want to go through debriefing with NASA. Doing more experiments with Sam Perkins didn't thrill them either as they knew nothing was going to happen; they just had to be there in case something did happen. It was not the happy go lucky atmosphere they'd had for the last few weeks. They were worried about outsiders, Mr. Perkins, and NASA. There was nothing they could do but keep up the pretense and go through the motions of doing experiments with hope in their voices and anticipation in their faces. No one could suspect, or they'd be relentless in their hounding of them until someone broke.

They all tried not to think of their success and where they'd be going or places and events they would see, because every time they thought of those things a smile would creep across their face and someone might catch them and know something was going on when they were supposedly so bummed, but still smiling.

Chapter 23

They were not even going to let them have breakfast their last morning. They'd be given breakfast back at headquarters.

Everyone was very upset at the turn of events, but inwardly they were sort of relieved that Mr. Perkins didn't stumble on the correct formula while fiddling around with their equipment. Denver walked to the small clearing about midnight and dug a hole wrapped the travel chairs in tarps, and buried the equipment to be retrieved in a couple years. He was an expert at camouflage, so you couldn't tell that anything had changed at all. He then went back to camp to sleep until the swift extraction they'd be receiving at first light.

No one was the wiser, yet everything was taken care of so NASA wouldn't be able to detect anything that would show up on their radar as suspicious.

They were all moping and weren't eager at all to leave. They did what they needed to do, but the NASA crew did most of the packing for departure. The commander kept prompting them and hurrying them, but he may as well not have been there. They just were sorry it was over and were showing it!

"All right everyone, I'm just as disappointed as you are, but we have no choice. We can't keep the helicopter circling and hovering much longer. You've got to pitch in and hurry up with packing your stuff before they decide to leave it." Tom announced. They expelled some moans and then really got busy, it was less than ten minutes before the last item was lifted and the chopper was on its way back to NASA headquarters.

Once they arrived, each individual's bin was taken to a specific area and they accompanied it to be searched and released.

The rest of the equipment was taken to another area for inspection and cataloging. If they took something that they didn't bring back or couldn't show proof of damage or consumption, there would be a major inquisition and it wouldn't even begin to measure what they would already have to go through. One team member went with each bin as witness that NASA wasn't claiming something missing that was actually there.

Alison chose to go with the food supplies and when they got to the fish, she asked if they could take it with them, since they caught them in the stream. She was told after they'd been opened, washed and declared clear of any contraband, they would release them to her. She wanted to arrange for them all to have dinner together that night and thought it would be nice to cook the fish. After they finished with the food supplies, they began on her personal bin. Once she was all cleared, and searched, they allowed her to leave. She was the third one released but the others were waiting near the entrance to the offices. They'd each been told their debriefing would begin the next day and they should all arrive by seven am, unless they were bunking at headquarters; then they could get up at six, dress and have breakfast. Alison was the only one who had family living close, so she invited them all for the fish dinner, but deemed to return to camp there with the others.

The dinner was great, as usual, she truly had a passion for cooking and it showed. They all laughed and talked some, but wrote down anything they needed to say about the internship. They were afraid they'd been bugged. Tom wrote first and he put "We did not achieve time travel. If we all believe that in our hearts, we can pass the polygraph." Everyone nodded and felt confident that they could keep their emotions in check about it to pass the test. Myra wrote "If we had more time, we might have gotten it worked out." Again they all nodded. Those were the two main points they had to believe without a doubt.

Alison destroyed the paper in the sink with a candle she had burning and then washed the ashes down the drain. No evidence of that conversation! They chatted some more and enjoyed the evening as much as possible. "I miss the campfire." Denver told them. They all had things they would miss, but the comradery they had with each other is what they'd miss the most. They'd gotten really close during that short amount of time, and they would miss each other a lot. "I want you all to promise to stay in touch with me." Margaret told them. "I need your friendship and value it very much." They all agreed with the sentiment as well as they wanted to stay in touch as well.

"Well, we'd better get back to headquarters." Steven said with a frown. "I just can't wait for debriefing to begin in the morning. I just wish I had positive results to tell them." He winked rather elaborately.

They all smiled and chimed in with "Me Too!" just in case big brother was listening.

Back at NASA they had two large bunkhouse type rooms. The three ladies were shown to beds in the one room, where four other women were already bunking and the men were shown to the other bunkhouse room where fifteen other men were occupying bunks. Each room could accommodate fifty so they had room to stretch out. They all unpacked their belongings and secured everything in the lockers that were provided with each bed. Since they had so much stuff and there were only seven women in their rooms, they each took two lockers. They figured someone there had master keys and could go through their stuff if they wanted to, so they were very careful not to leave anything in there that could question their experiments. Not that they'd saved anything that could. They'd done full examinations of all their stuff once they'd decided to leave NASA out in the cold. They made themselves as comfortable as possible and went to sleep.

Well it wasn't a helicopter waking them at six am, but it was a very loud buzzer sounding throughout the entire complex. The whole place came alive in a matter of minutes. Everyone had a routine to do and their team was no exception. They got dressed and made their way to the cafeteria for breakfast. It was ok, but nothing like they'd been eating in the mountains. It was a whole lot of pre-cooked or pre-prepared foods. It was edible, but the company made it enjoyable. "Does anyone know what time and who's being debriefed first?" Alan asked as Tom walked up. "Seems like we all are going to be at the same time in different rooms, I guess they think we'll talk it over and come up with 'stories' to tell. I, myself, don't have time for such foolishness and neither do any of you, I'd wager." He smiled. "Anyway, they'll be coming here to get us at seven and take us to our respective partners for debriefing. I'll be glad to get it over with myself; and get back to a lab somewhere so I can make a real difference in the world. Or hope to anyway; since that wasn't the end result of this experiment anyway." He finished.

'Don't take it so hard Doc, we were making progress and had we not been sabotaged, I'm sure we'd have found the right power or the correction needed in the calculations." George assured him.

They'd finished eating and were talking when a very official group entered the cafeteria, ten of them to be exact. One of them for each member of their team. Their leader announced that one of the team should go with one of their team. It didn't matter which as they were just getting their stories down and asking their opinions and questions about things they tried. They also wanted them to do a survey on the efficiency of the NASA team taking them in and bringing them out. Just simple stuff, but once we review everyone's reports, we may have questions as to why something was left out of a particular person's report or such. They turned to leave and a member of Tom's team fell in line behind each member of NASA's team and followed them to different rooms where the interrogation would begin.

They started out with simple stuff, asking about their food, the camp, if everything was sufficient or less than the quality they needed. Then they moved on to the actual experiments. The team members tried to remember as best they could what order they tried the different powers and what the result was with each. Every one of them reminded their interrogator that there was at least one video of every combination they'd tried, some there were more. That would help them determine what order it all was in. They just wanted the team to do the best they could to give the details from memory versus the video; but the videos would be examined as well.

They began telling little things that were unique to each of them. For instance how Margaret fed the squirrels extra nuts on the days they were going to be in experiments. She felt guilty that the poor things were being fried and they had no control over it. Or about the time when their laundry was sabotaged by a raccoon and it all had to be rewashed as he'd chewed through the rope and everything hit the ground. They'd replaced the rope with wire to eliminate that issue. Or when Mr. Perkins came in stumbling over everything in the camp in the middle of the night and woke them all up, sending every single team member out of their tents with the biggest thing they could grab to clobber something or someone. The close scare they had with the mama bear and her cubs. How they'd tear out the beaver dam and the next day the beavers would have it built right back. They talked about the dinners near the campfire and popcorn or s'mores made over that fire. How they'd made an oven out of a log and a covered iron skillet so they could have baked goods. They talked about singing as Denver played his guitar and of course how they appreciated the wireless internet every evening so they could keep in touch with their friends and families. They bragged about the diversity of the food they'd been supplied with and how amazingly it had been prepared each day. How it all seemed to taste better cooked outside. Their stories overlapped one another's so the examiners would see they were true. They were true stories and they were all stories that each of them loved. They'd grown close on that mountain and enjoyed every minute of each other's company. When they talked about those things, it was genuine and you could tell it by listening and looking at them. It showed in their faces.

Every single one of them recounted the experiment with the magnetic energy and how they had the loud bang and the squirrel was gone. They'd been so sure he'd gone into the future and had begun congratulating each other on finding it, when someone turned around and burst into laughter when they saw the squirrel. And of course how everyone was in stitches over it all once they realized that the magnet had sucked the squirrel backwards so fast that the team, whose eyes were trained forward, couldn't even tell it had passed behind them and had not been projected into the future at all.

They told about making perfume and how they'd all worked together to make a fishing rig that actually caught enough fish for two meals for everyone; and some of them were hearty eaters. They recounted their terror at the laser accident that damaged trees and a mountain along with their fear at being discovered because of it; but then having to leave early anyway. They made sure NASA understood their sadness at not achieving their goal and each expressed their desire for another shot.

They told them how amazed they were with the precision and expertise of their agents. They were always on time, exactly on time, and they were professional and extremely motivated. They could load and unload a helicopter faster than a normal team of twenty. They were amazing to watch.

They each expressed their love of the West Virginia mountains, the flowers, vegetation and the animals that roamed freely. They were all students at West Virginia University, but they hadn't really be out in the middle of nowhere before and it was relaxing and peaceful. They'd had no illnesses or allergy issues like they did when they went to a big city somewhere.

They all told of their relationship with the professor, how he made them feel as equals and was a delight to work with. He got excited, but never flustered or irate with anyone except Mr. Perkins. He was furious when he blew that hole in the mountain. Other than that, he was extremely mild mannered and such a gentleman.

They, in turn, expressed how they thought they'd be lonely or feel lost out there, but it was almost like home or a reunion with their friends. Another amazing fact since most of them hadn't met each other and none had met Dr. Livingston, who was amazing by the way. She was a gentle doctor and knew modern medicine and home remedies just as well. They all liked her too.

Once they steered them back to the more technical parts of their trip, they talked more about different things and parts of the experiments. They discussed in detail things they remembered about each experiment, like a wire coming unconnected, or putting the magnet away after that incident. It was so charged, everything metal was being pulled toward it. They covered it with several tarps and put it in the bin too, and it would still pull metal towards it, if you got to close.

They talked about the things in history they'd hoped to witness first hand had they been able to time travel. That was the stuff dreams were made of and until Mr. Perkins got there and shattered them all, they were still dreaming of the things they'd see and the places they would go.

They told them about the weather there, the chilly evenings and the hot days. They told about the storm that was on top of them before they had a clue it was anywhere near that big and bad. How it came and went and really didn't do much more than make their hair stand up from the static electricity running through the ground from the lightning and the good drenching they got from it.

They told about the hikes they took and how wonderful the swims were in the creek. They each seemed to really go way off track when the examiner asked anything personal or about anything other than the experiments. It was like they would tell every little detail about a squirrel, trying to wear down their inquisitor before they themselves were worn down.

Tom told them the champagne he'd taken to celebrate their accomplishment was still packed, unopened, as they'd not gotten to have their celebration.

This interrogation went on for a week before NASA released them with instructions that they may be calling with any questions they came up with once they had compared everyone's recollection of the events of the internship. They would examine the videos, the notes, and all the stories. It would probably take them another week, so they should plan on being available for more questioning shortly after that.

They all hugged, gathered their stuff and headed toward their respective destinations. Most were going back to school. Tom was going back to Mike's.

NASA had installed bugs in all their clothes and on their suitcases. Tom had placed small notes in each of their hands as they shook hands and said goodbye, telling them to stop and buy a new outfit and rent a locker to put all their stuff in and leave it there for six months before retrieving it and destroying nearly everything that couldn't be physically debugged. They didn't need the added worry of someone picking up on something they'd said. They all already knew to be careful, but they needed to be extra careful since NASA didn't get what they wanted.

The students traveled back together in two cars so there were lots of notes being passed around, especially when they stopped for meals. Denver knew a way to disable the bugs. He used a magnetic field which worked for most bugs, but the military stuff was higher grade and you had to go the extra mile with radiation. Denver had a friend who was a chiropractor, so they stopped at his office, changed into examining gowns and put everything they owned through his x-ray machine. He then used a meter to check some of them, and none were emitting any electrical pulses at all. They knew they were clean then, except for the car. They were sure it was bugged as well.

Life would be different for a while, probably a long while.

As each member was dropped off at his or her destination, they each bid that one farewell and assured each other they would keep in touch. They all knew their code words to use should they need to really talk or were having an issue that required help. They would be living life as if they'd failed in their experiments. Those graduating would be pursuing their respective goals in life and their careers. They nearly all talked daily, just to keep in touch and check on one another and at least monthly they skyped altogether so they could see each other's faces and catch up with a long conversation. They also held up notes for the others to read so things didn't need to be said. They'd usually ask Denver to play something for them and that's when they'd disclose whatever it was they wanted to share or needed help with so it didn't have to be a conversation and so anyone listening in would not wonder why no one was talking. They didn't want them to figure out the reason was everyone was reading. It worked really well and they did enjoy his guitar music too. He even recorded a couple songs so he could play them and join in on the conversation with his own notes and paper questions.

Tom told them he was laying his work aside for a year. It was hard and killing him. He wanted to check and recheck everything for the millionth time, but he felt if he came back after a year and looked again, he might see whatever he was not seeing now. They all agreed that made sense; and were hoping to eliminate some of the scrutiny they were under, but it really didn't work.

It seemed they'd be watched for several years, but that was ok with them. They knew what was waiting and they knew it was secure. They could wait. Alison told them she'd started taking nuts to the local park to feed the squirrels, she just felt so guilty for destroying so many of them. There were a dozen regulars who recognized her when she entered the park, even the few times she'd gone with someone and didn't have nuts with her, so she knew it wasn't the nuts they were smelling. They either recognized her scent or her face. She wasn't sure how squirrels worked, but thought she might start doing some research on animals for fun and she was taking more classes to further her interests in power sources and ways to pump up the power from the original source and develop sustainable natural power sources. Everyone congratulated her for her way of thinking. She, after all did love working with power and she had begun to feel better about the squirrels, even if she couldn't go to the park without some nuts for fear of being attacked. They were greedy little creatures and persistant. The few times she didn't have anything for them, they stood up and gave her a lecture, just chattering and shaking their arms and fists at her. She imagined if they could talk, she'd have burning ears. She liked to watch them though and was definitely going to do that research on their communication habbits.

Denver had gotten hired by NASA and Margaret was hired by the Department of Defense. They were both thrilled with their dream jobs and were right where they wanted to be, working on the things that interested them the most. Never a boring day at the job when you loved what you were doing.

George got a job as Vice President of product development at a major pharmaceutical company.

Alan was hired by a medical equipment company. He was in charge of robotic prosthetics development. He felt that would be the most rewarding thing he could do and still enjoy the geek side of working in that field.

Steven, Ryan and Jody were going after their Masters degrees, so they'd see a lot of each other over the course of time. They'd have classes together and would probably all secure top level teaching positions at the elite colleges and universities.

Myra went back to teaching at the university. It was truly her passion to teach up and coming doctors. She loved every minute of it and was a great teacher too. She had that rapport with her students. They loved and trusted her and with that connection, they delved deep into their studies and excelled in her classes; which was very rewarding in its own right.

Chapter 24

It had been three years since NASA sent them home. They'd all gone about their business like nothing had ever happened or would happen with time travel.

They were finally beginning to relax, but would never take any chances either with any information they had in their brains or by commenting on anything they'd done. As far as everyone was concerned, it was a failed experiment and they intended it to stay that way no matter how long NASA dogged them about it.

Tom petitioned every year to NASA for another opportunity to study and experiment. He wanted to keep up pretenses, so he'd file all the paperwork, make recommendations and ask for their opinions and recommendations for further trials and/or calculations.

Denver had gone back to the **Laurel Fork Federal Wilderness in West Virginia** and retrieved the two chairs with the control boxes. He had stored them in the storage unit they'd secured in their future, which was now their present. He retrieved them while he was home visiting his parents and then dropped them off at the unit on the way back to NASA. He parked his car and then paid cash to rent a vehicle to drive to the storage unit. He knew the guy at the rental place so they let him do that without a credit card to hold and nothing went through the system. It was untraceable, so he felt safe in the process of doing that. No one would think he could do that, so they wouldn't dig any further than the customary credit card check.

They had decided on their last skype that they would wait another six months before doing any time traveling. They were getting so close, it would be tough waiting any longer. They all wanted to do it so badly, they could taste it.

Tom had begun traveling right after that skype meeting, but he hadn't told anyone and he always came back within a minute of the time he'd left so no one would find him missing for any length of time. He was not changing anything or affecting anyone's lives; he was merely traveling all over the world, witnessing life and occasionally a historical event. He had to be extra careful not to be witnessed in any photographs or on television. That would destroy all their well-played stories.

He had accumulated a vast assortment of costumes he used for each era and country he visited. He'd gleaned a few secrets along the way. This was the most fascinating part of time travel. Finding out for yourself if history was recorded correctly or filling in the blanks or gaps where history failed to record enough information. For instance he knew who actually killed Lincoln and the conspiracy involved in the cover-up. He'd witnessed alien contact at Area 51. Now that one left him with some eerie feelings and a few bad dreams afterwards. That was another thing that didn't seem possible, but he'd witnessed it and knew for certain that it was. He knew who had the missing minutes of the Watergate tapes. He was there when OJ's wife was murdered as well as Jon Benet Ramsey. Those were two of the most publicized murders other than presidents. He watched Jack The Ripper leave the house of Mary Kelly, so he was the only one who knew for sure who he was; well except for those powers that got him off and covered it up. There always seemed to be those powers behind the scenes who had all the power and used it to their own means and whims.

It was easy to discover things going back since he knew the date, place and time of the events. It was just a hop, skip and a leap back to that exact location and time and then just keep your eyes and ears open to discover all the secrets, most of which were dirty secrets, thus the secrecy of it all and the purposeful leaving out of information to the general public.

He witnessed the building of the great pyramid, and the Sphinx. He was there at the destruction of Sodom and Gomorrah and the great flood of Noah. Well, he watched until the flood was two thirds the way up the mountain he was watching from before he left. That one took a few tries to get it right as he didn't want to travel into the midst of the flood. He needed to go several years prior and estimate how long they still had to go and try again at that time. His fourth attempt was in the midst of the animals being loaded. Now that was an amazing sight to see. They just came willingly to the ark and were led in without a growl or anything. That made him a believer in a higher power being in control of this world. He knew God existed from that alone, without any scientific evidence. The fifth attempt was hours before the floodgates were opened.

He'd watched the beatings, the trial, and the crucifixion of Christ. That one took him days to recover from. It wasn't the travel, it was the gravity of seeing it all. He'd wept bitterly there at the cross and after he'd returned home. It changed him for the better, but he was a very different man after that. He was much more concerned with what he could do to help mankind. The starving people of the world, the sick and dying were top on his list of those needing him. He became a devout Christian and witnessed to people of Christ. He wasn't proud of his lies to NASA, but he knew God was accepting of it due to the nature of the government, should they discover the means to defy time and place.

He'd seen the Eifel tower being built, worked at the Hoover Dam build site, helped with the underground railroad, witnessed the signing of the Declaration of Independence and watched Ben Franklin harness electricity. It was a pleasure for him to spend time with Thomas Edison and Henry Ford. He met Louis XIV and Cleopatra. When one of the people he wanted to meet popped into his head, he'd gather his costume and start plans to go see them. It caused him to jump all over the world in various years and eras, but it was so thrilling he didn't care. He was a sponge and was soaking everything up as fast as he could. He was a first-hand witness to some of the greatest events in history. He could debunk a lot of wrong analogies about a lot of subjects. He could clear up unsolved mysteries and settle 1000 year old arguments; if he could only speak up. Then no one would believe him, so it didn't matter. He was privileged and honored to get to see it all fist hand. If he never did anything else in life, he'd die a happy man.

His favorite personal thing he had done so far was

to visit his family in the past. He told them what he'd done and explained they couldn't tell anyone and why. He didn't want to put anyone in jeopardy, but he loved them and missed them so terribly he just had to go home. They were thrilled to see him, especially his mother. He got a good look at himself from a distance. He didn't dare interfere with his own existence; but he had. He just didn't know it at the time. He didn't think about his wonderful mother giving him the ideas about time travel when he was a child, explaining to him the possibility of it all being real. The moment he got home from that trip, he realized that his mother had instilled in him the desire to pursue this dream. She'd told him of adventures he would have once he'd achieved time travel. She made it something he greatly desired to do from the stories she told him about history and the travels he would make. She was the one who urged him to enter the field of science and kept reminding him of his dream. She encouraged him for years to pursue his heart's dream. He didn't remember any of that until now. Not because he'd forgotten, but because it had really just happened. He had no memories of this because he'd just caused them all with the visit to his mother. Would he have discovered time travel had he not gone back to visit his mother? From the way the memories seemed to appear after he returned, he doubted it very much. It was a variable with time and history he hadn't thought of. The trip had made them both so very happy, regardless of how it affected his life after that. It felt good to be in her tight hug once again and to seek her advice on life and anything he should do with the rest of his life. He told her about his newfound faith and his trip back in time.

Suddenly he recalled that his mother had started taking him to church quite often and had declared to anyone who would listen that the whole Bible was true and no one could convince her otherwise. He decided that was due to his visit as well. Maybe his returning home saved her soul. He knew his time traveling had saved his. No one could have convinced him that the Bible was 100% true had he not witnessed parts of it himself. He was a scientist and they normally needed concrete evidence; but Tom had learned about faith.

There really was no way to have interaction with anyone in the past and not have it affect the present or future in some way or another. He'd remember that on future travels. He'd be more careful than ever about avoiding contact or not saying anything that could make someone form an opinion that would have originated with him.

He would, however keep traveling through time and learning first-hand what history had recorded and how history sometimes got it wrong. He would also caution his team about how easy a single word could change a future event. They'd have to carefully weigh every situation before they even went to that time and place. The balance of time and history could be shifted so easily and there would be ten of them traveling around.

He had built small packs that held the control box and power source so that they wouldn't have to have a car or chair, they could just hold it in their hand, wear it like a belt, or sling it over their shoulder once the timer was set and the coordinates put in. Whichever way it blended in with their era clothing so it wouldn't be questioned.

The ladies could put it in their purses. It was pretty small, but oh so powerful! They were going to be so impressed. They didn't really need the apparatus around them for protection as sometimes a car would be too big to fit where they were trying to land. They would just need to be careful of their footing as they emerged into the future or past. It was much less conspicuous than a car or a chair. He did still use them, depending on when and where he was going. He regularly visited the 50's and every time, he took the car. He loved the drive-in, sock hops, malt shops, the clothes, hamburger stands and especially the music. It was a real treat to actually do the twist with Chubby Checker. He was a major history buff and loved watching it all unfold, but some aspects of time travel were for the sheer joy of it all. Tom was certainly having a ball and loving every trip he made. Even the hard ones to witness gave him deep insight to how people think and act during different periods of their lives and how power changes everyone. He often worried how the others would react to their travels, but felt they were a good bunch and he would caution them again and again about being careful and not being seen. The only way to remain anonymous in history was to blend in. He always looked like a regular Joe, nothing stood out about him and he acted exactly like every other citizen of that time period and that came from some good research on each place before he left.

He was looking forward to seeing the whole gang back together again. He had a huge list of things to go over with them and of course many many things to show them and even more things to tell them of his adventures. Things they could go and see for themselves, or just accept his story and spend their time elsewhere. He knew they would all want to start traveling as soon as possible and if there wasn't anything suspicious going on during their stay, then they would all be able to take their packs home with them after some initial travels together so there were no questions or problems. He knew there wouldn't be because he'd tested every single pack, but he wanted them to be comfortable as well. He could only imagine the places they would all go. Many of the places he'd enjoy, but many places that were very personal to each of them as well.

They would be arriving tomorrow, so Tom had to get busy preparing for their visits. First of all he had to get some food in the house. He took care of his chores and headed to bed early that night as he knew he'd have a busy exciting day tomorrow.

They began arriving early, which Tom attributed to their excitement building up to actually traveling in time. A couple came together, but most arrived separately within minutes of each other. It was only two hours between the first and the last to arrive. Everyone was talking at once to whoever would listen. They needed to catch up and dispel some of the energy built up in them. They just couldn't hold it any longer.

Finally when the last one arrived, Tom had lunch ready, so they all sat down to eat and talk. He'd asked them to keep it to small chit-chat over lunch and then they'd get into the details of what they all wanted to do most. Over the next six hours they discussed and documented when, where, why and who wanted to go to about two hundred different places. That was the beginning of their lists. Tom told them his details and how he'd had not a single problem or glitch. He also explained about his mother and cautioned them again how anything and everything said or done would actually cause ripples in time and change things down the road.

They all agreed if anything was at all out of order or suspicious, they would contact him as quickly as possible to discuss what could have occurred and what they'd need to do to fix it. Anything that caused a change in history would have to be fixed immediately or everything about their history could change and thus affect their futures. It was a tightrope they were walking and one mishap could change the world, and maybe not for the better.

They decided to go out to dinner and enjoy each other's company before they headed into the past before bedtime. They called Tom's favorite restaurant and they said they could accommodate their party, so they were off and it was to be Tom's treat. They had a delightful evening and dinner was exquisite. Tom suggested they take the two cars and head off to the 50's for a movie at the drive-in since none of them had gotten to experience that before. They donned their outfits, the guys slicked back their hair, rolled up their jeans and pulled on their leather jackets over their white t-shirts. They all looked perfect and were so excited. It was a good movie and the popcorn and sodas were a big hit with everyone. When the fun was over, they came home and talked another three hours before they decided they'd better get to bed. It was after all two o'clock in the morning.

The next day, after much more cautioning by Tom,

they all began to go their separate ways with their own personal time travel pack.

They couldn't wait to start traveling on their own and exploring the world past, present, and future.

Myra was a little scared to go on her own so she made sure to be the last one to leave so she could ask Tom to go with her. "I'm just afraid I won't be able to stand idly by and not help someone who's dying when I could save their life. I know it would alter history, but I'm a doctor and I don't know if I could do it or not, especially if I'm there by myself with no one to jump in and stop me. If I were to find someone choking and do the Heimlich maneuver on them and it was before Heimlich discovered it, then history would change. It may not be safe to let me go alone. Can I just meet you places and you keep me in check. I have so many things I want to witness, but I certainly don't want to mess up. Please." She asked. Tom assured her that would be fine with him as they got along so well anyway, it would be a pleasure to escort her through time. He thought it would be a better experience if someone in the know were with him anyway. So they set a schedule and coordinates to meet at and then they could go where she wanted to go.

They'd been traveling three to four times per week for about six months when the unthinkable happened. Tom was spotted reappearing by a NASA agent. It was less than a blink between the time he left and then returned from a travel, but it was enough for the agent to wonder if his eyes had deceived him or not. He was there on a routine spot check but after that he started watching Tom's activities more closely. He'd decided he would be watching Tom every possible minute of every day, as he was trying to make a name for himself at NASA. If his suspicions were correct everyone there would know his name. Peter McNally would be a household name for sure. He'd also planted a couple bugs when Tom left for the grocery store one day and he'd searched the house then and any chance he could when Tom would go out to eat or leave for what looked like any amount of time. He managed to plant six cameras and had started filming Tom. What he noticed was there were times that he seemed to glitch, sort of like he was on the film, was not, but in less than a blink, he was again. Once he was convinced, he took it to NASA's team who dissected it frame by frame and found there was a millisecond that Tom truly was not there. That's when they decided he must have discovered time travel and that minuscule amount of time he was off film, was when he was traveling.

The guy searched and searched, but could find no evidence of any apparatus that could be used for time travel and there was none that could be seen in the films. Whatever he was using to travel had to be with him all the time. Apparently Tom was carrying it so it wouldn't be found at his home. That would be even easier to find then. He'd have Tom arrested and all his possessions would be confiscated and held until he was released. He would get a court order to search his possessions while he was being held. It was brilliant. He couldn't believe Tom had actually done it, but this had to be proof of it and he wasn't going to let this go. He couldn't go to the top dogs yet, as he didn't have enough information or evidence, so he'd have to find some somewhere and this was a great place to look since he'd checked every place in Tom's house.

He contacted the judge they used for surveillance and secured the court order to search Tom's personal belongings and house at any time day or night under the national security act. If Tom had indeed completed time travel he could definitely be a threat to national security. He then requested an arrest order for Tom to be picked up for questioning in a national security matter. When Tom was brought in, Peter was practically drooling. He knew his prey was caught and all he had to do was check all his belongings and then call the big brass to tell them what he'd discovered.

Unfortunately for Mr. McNally, there was nothing to be found and he'd tipped his hand to Tom. He made sure they turned his house upside down before they released him. They found nothing. When they questioned Tom, he stuck with his original story that he'd not had adequate time to fine tune and make enough adjustments to his equations for everything to work. The experiments had been a flop and since NASA would no longer fund the research, it had been abandoned.

Peter grilled Tom about discovering time travel and every time he said anything about it, Tom would deny it and explain how nothing worked. He'd reminded him how everyone there would have known had they achieved their goal and they'd already cleared everyone.

McNally was a rookie though and overly eager to climb the ladder at NASA and he tipped his hand. He told Tom he had video proof that he had traveled in time. He had it on film and it had already been analyzed by NASA. There was a millisecond that he disappeared from the video and then was back. Tom told him it could have been a power surge, or drop in power would have caused the video to malfunction for a millisecond's worth of recording time. Tom asked him if it was just one time he found this or over and over. McNally told him it was just one time. "Well there you have it!" Tom told him. "Believe you me, if I had the technology to travel through time, I'd be doing it all the time. I'd be somewhere right now. You would find me missing all the time, and not just for a millisecond either. I'd be gone for days, weeks, or even months living it up around the world in every time you could imagine. Has that been the case with your surveillance?" he asked. McNally had to admit that it had not happened again and he supposed it could have been a glitch in the filming, but he would be keeping an eye on Tom from now on. Tom reminded him that could be considered harassment since they'd not found any proof that he'd done anything wrong, nor had he been placed on any homeland security lists as a threat. He might just have to check with his attorney about what action he might need to take against him for harassment and any other charges the attorney might be inclined to pursue.

Peter could not believe his misfortune and now he had to give account to his superiors regarding his actions in falsely accusing a pillar of the community.

Tom's phone call from jail was to George Duncan. He was afraid to call Denver since he was working for NASA. He didn't want to cause him any undo stress or security issues.

George came and got him from jail and they took his house room by room, scanning and removing all bugs and cameras. Tom said he'd clean up and put everything back later since they'd seemed to pretty much trash the place—not destructive, but they'd thrown his stuff everywhere.

Finally when they were sure everything was safe for talking important stuff; George asked him where his device was for traveling since they were obviously looking for it and hadn't found it. Tom laughed and explained he'd been working on that for quite a while now and had developed an extremely small device in a ball point pen case. They had it in their hands, but it was also a fully functioning pen so they didn't notice anything wrong or different about it. The guy was too power hungry to think about what he really needed to do to find it, or he'd have brought scanners for power output, like Geiger counters and magnetic detectors, etc. He showed George how it worked. Once the pen was disassembled, you could see the numbers for setting the time, date, and place coordinates. They were small, but easy enough to change without a magnifying glass. The amount of plutonium truly needed to power the trip was much less than they'd originally thought and Tom had kept decreasing the size of it until it fit nicely inside the pen. Now the pen was not the slim line ones, but had the bigger bottom for a comfortable grip. Fortunately he'd worked hard on it and had everything else hidden in the storage unit; or NASA would have him in jail and all his data, cars, plutonium, the chairs and the belts they'd made for travel. He just hadn't gotten all the team their pens yet. He almost had them engraved, but decided something from him might be scrutinized should anyone decide to put any of them through what he'd been put through.

He and George discussed their next plan of action and decided if they could find the date Peter had seen Tom's glitch, then they could go back and stop it all from happening. Tom would just not make the trip that time and they would all know to still be on the lookout and to make sure they returned at the exact second they'd departed so nothing could be detected. They'd be using their new pen devices as well, so nothing would be noticed on any of them. Tom had to get Myra's to her right away so her belt device could be put in storage, leaving nothing for NASA to find should they decide to search her place next.

They called Denver to see if he could get a copy of McNally's report so they'd have a closer date to start with, but he said he couldn't do it due to suspicions already placed on him. He'd have a hard time traveling himself, but with the new device it would be much more feasible for him to proceed. They told him they understood and asked if he had a date to suggest. They thought maybe when McNally suddenly wasn't in the office a lot. Denver thought on that during their whole conversation and in the middle of one of George's sentences burst out with "I've got a date! He wasn't at the annual awards banquet. He was up for something and when they announced his name, his supervisor said he was in the field. So I'd start prior to that date. Why don't you guys see if you can get a copy of the request for the warrant, it may have a date that the first suspicion was raised. Since you were innocent, you may be able to request the report from NASA yourself. It's worth a shot since your civil liberties were violated. Just tell them you want it to see what all he did to your house prior to the arrest and what McNally had found to cause you to be placed on the watch list for national security. You'd like to be exonerated from all charges and need to know every suspicion that was raised. If they give you the right to the file, ask for any recordings, video and audio. You may catch it yourself and be able to go back and eliminate the original cause leaving no record of anything with NASA or any other agency. I think it's imperative you get this part of history changed as it will come back to haunt us all. Some other hotshot will come across the file and start another investigation and may include us all. We're as careful as we can be, but we don't always think about someone watching us in our own homes. I think we need to do sweeps for bugs and cameras every month. I'll pick up what's needed, they're not very expensive and when we all get together for dinner next week; I'll hand them out when everyone gets their pens."

They had their plans and each set their sights on making it all happen. George was on one line with NASA while Tom was on with the local police dept. about the arrest warrant. Of course Tom had to speak with the NASA representative, but George was certainly getting them to that point. Once Tom took over with NASA, George set about calling the other team members to confirm the dinner. Supposedly both agencies would be sending the files and information.

George suggested that they canvas Tom's neighborhood to see if anyone saw the guy in his car or the bushes. Anything suspicious could help them narrow the time down as well. They started with the closest houses and would work their way down the street. George crossed the street to start on that side and hit the jackpot the very first door he knocked on. An elderly lady lived there and had been a school teacher. She had a habit of writing things down and she nearly had a book on the guy they were looking for. She described him and went back in to get her book. While she was getting it, George called for Tom to come over. They explained to her about the guy bringing up charges against Tom and how they were trying to figure out what caused the suspicion to start with. She found the first date she'd seen him there and noted a couple times she'd seen him enter Tom's house after Tom had left for an errand. She saw him carry a briefcase in, which was probably when he had placed the cameras and bugs in the house. She had the date they were looking for too. On that night, she explained that he was watching and stepped out from behind the tree to get a better look, wiped his eyes and looked again. It was just after that he started going in the house. She took them over to the tree he would hide behind and they saw the grass had been worn off and even a cigarette butt was on the ground. They picked it up and put it in a bag to check for DNA. Tom asked her to please let him know if she saw suspicious things like that in the future or if she was ever scared by something or someone outside and he'd come over to check on her and make sure she was safe. She thanked him and said she was sorry she didn't let him know before but she'd tried a few years back with someone else and they didn't believe her, said she was just a busybody trying to stir up trouble. She assured him she wasn't, but was leery about speaking up now that she'd been scolded for her efforts. Tom and George thanked her several more times and assured her she'd been a great help. As they were leaving, she stopped them and explained she hadn't even told them her name. They smiled and she introduced herself as Mrs. Agnes Carnes. Tom shook her hand and thanked her again. He also asked if it would be ok for him to visit her occasionally to make sure she was doing ok. Maybe they'd sit on the porch and watch the neighborhood together. She said she'd like that very much. She was quite a bit older than Tom so she knew it was just a nice neighborly thing he was doing, but she also knew she'd enjoy his company. Tom was pretty sure he'd enjoy her's as well. She was quite entertaining. She was pleasant, but she watched their neighborhood like a hawk. She knew everybody's business, but didn't really stick her nose in any of it or share it with anyone. She wasn't a gossip, she just didn't have anything to do after her husband had passed and all her kids were grown and had moved away. She was lonely so she watched everyone else live their lives. It was sort of sad, but it kept her busy and that was the main thing. He and so many other people missed so much by not befriending people like her. She'd lived a lot of life and held a wealth of knowledge that could help most people and keep them from making the wrong decisions about a lot of things if they could just learn their lessons from her instead of having to make their own mistakes.

Well if they could match that date with the NASA and police reports they should be able to start pretty close to the right day, unless they were lucky enough for that day to be in McNally's report to NASA. At least they'd have ammunition to fight with in securing the reports if they weren't forthcoming. It was a good day and they both felt they'd accomplished a lot.

Now to get ready for the dinner; they had four days to plan everything and get the food and supplies in that were needed for it. George would be returning home after the dinner, but would assist Tom with securing the documents and traveling back to help change history if his help was needed. If he stayed much longer, he was afraid they'd become more suspicious of them trying to hide something.

As promised, the reports arrived two days later and Tom and George were as excited as little kids on Christmas morning. The audio and video tapes were not in the packets, but they didn't really expect them. They knew NASA would have locked them away or destroyed them totally as there would be date stamps which was exactly what Tom had wanted. They read the reports and McNally had listed the date he began gathering data on Tom and he also listed the date he'd secured the warrant for the cameras and bugs to be installed. They were golden—this was exactly what they needed and along with Mrs. Carnes records, they should be able to change everything in one or two tries at the most. They planned the counter intelligence efforts down to the second. Not only did Tom plan on not making that trip, but George was going to cause a disturbance to distract Mr. McNally so he wouldn't catch the glitch if they happened to choose the wrong time Tom had traveled and was spotted.

They would do it that night so they'd know if all was well before the team arrived for their much anticipated dinner at Tom's. They were hoping it would be as easy to fix as it seemed it would be, but set themselves to not be too disappointed should they fail on the first attempt. They executed their plan. George went back to an hour before McNally should have arrived and told the Tom in the past the plan. He then left and positioned himself down the street to set up the distraction. At the precise minute Tom would have traveled originally, George made a very loud commotion with some trash cans in the alley just past where McNally was lurking. McNally was distracted and Tom didn't make the trip at all, so there was no trace of anything on any film that McNally would have had showing a glitch. He did stand in the spot he had left from, but then moved on to the living room to sit and watch TV.

George watched McNally until he left that night and then walked to Tom's, went in and he discussed with Tom how he thought it had worked and how he would be transporting back to the future from the darkened bedroom so no one would see him traveling either.

When George arrived back at Tom's after they'd done what they could to avert McNally's investigation, they had to figure out a way to determine if they'd fixed the problem or not. They thought for a while and then it hit him. Check with Mrs. Carnes. If it had worked, they wouldn't have gone to her for her help in clearing his name. She wouldn't even know who Tom was as they'd never have met.

It was just after nine o'clock so he decided it wouldn't be too late to ring her bell. He was sure she'd be up for the eleven o'clock news. He needed a reason to be there so he figured he'd make up a commotion happening on that night. When she came to the door, Tom explained that he was just there to check on her since there was a big commotion down the alley and didn't want her to be afraid. She told him she hadn't heard the commotion, but thanked him through the door and was turning to leave when Tom introduced himself and asked her name. He apologized for not having met her before now, but he had seen her in the yard once and knew she was elderly and alone and that's why he checked on her. He gave her his number and said any time she needed help or was scared, just give him a call and he'd check on her. He even suggested they visit occasionally for lemonade or tea, depending on the weather and it would give them both a little company if she thought that would be ok. She was delighted and expressed her gratitude and appreciation for her newfound friend. He told her he was looking forward to it, that neighbors should get to know one another. They would be there if needed, but not be a nuisance to anyone. Just friends if they could be.

Tom nearly skipped back across the road to his house. It had worked! She had no clue who he was and McNally had seen nothing out of the ordinary. They decided Tom should confront him the next time he was lurking around. He could use Mrs. Carnes as his excuse. Maybe he'd get the hint that he was being watched as well and move along since he hadn't found anything anyway.

Chapter 25

The team arrived right on time for dinner. Denver had gotten there first and swept Tom's house for bugs and cameras and had found none. The return to the past had definitely worked. He did a sweep of everyone after they'd come in, along with their purses, and coats. Then they got down to explaining to the others what had happened and how they believed it had been fixed. They each received their new devices to detect the bugs and their new traveling devices. They were all so excited, especially once they saw how small they were and yet still easy to use. Tom cautioned everyone to depart and return to a dark place in their houses so any video wouldn't be able to pick them up. Act like they were going to bed, or the bathroom. It didn't matter as long as they couldn't be seen because they would be returning the same second they left. This way they wouldn't raise any suspicions of why they were ten hours in the bathroom. They could travel for as long as they wanted, years even, but they had to return at the same second they'd departed.

They all agreed that was easy enough and confirmed they remembered all their prior precautions that had been given about appropriate clothing, blending in, etc. This was the best gifts they'd received in their lives. He cautioned them to travel to the storage unit and leave their belt packs there as they would be too easy to detect during a search or detainment as he'd endured. Had he not had his new device everything would have been destroyed. He didn't know when one of them might be targeted for observation and/or wire-tapping, searches, etc.

They were excited to find out what Tom had in store for them for dinner and for after dinner as well.

Tom and George had actually cooked dinner, grilled steaks with some very fancy vegetables done on the grill as well, hot rolls and salad. Yum was the word of the hour as they all knew how good that was going to be.

After dinner I thought we would all go see one of the following:
      Eruption of Mount Vesuvius
      The Titanic hit the iceberg
      The Hindenburg Explode
A little risky and sad for the people involved, but wow, to be there to experience it! Or if you want a calmer, yet amazing evening we can see the Aura Borealis in Alaska

Everyone opted for the Eruption of Mount Vesuvius almost in unison, so we thought we'd do that and then go straight to Alaska for some beauty after seeing all the desolation in Pompeii.

Actually when it was all said and done; they traveled to all four destinations that night. They didn't want the night to end or their experiences either. It was quite the debate as to which was better, the Hindenburg or the Titanic. Better to be on either to enjoy the luxury of the time; but safer traveling home before the Titanic began to sink and traveling from the Hindenburg to the ground below just before it exploded and watching it come down.

They arrived at the Titanic three hours before they hit the iceberg, so they enjoyed the dancing and after dinner desserts that were offered. The dressing up in the period costumes was fun for everyone, but especially the ladies. They made sure to go above deck just a few minutes before it hit so they could watch it collide and the flurry of people and activities before it began to sink. They couldn't stay to watch it go down as they would not let the men in the boats to escape, but they were in the thrill of the moment and they were able to ride on the Hindenburg and time travel to the ground just before it exploded.

They both were amazing works of mechanical engineering, but sadly they both seemed cursed by their makers. They all felt that one shouldn't toot one's own horn too loudly or too often. Those men thought they were above God and God just doesn't like that and tends to make or allow things to happen to bring folks like that down where they belong. You know, knock them off their own pedestal. Anyway they all knew they would never be that egotistical. They all felt blessed to be in this group and to be able to do the things they were doing.

They were all going to spend the night and head to their respective homes in the morning. It had been a glorious night and they vowed to do it again, at least twice a year. Traveling all together was even more fun and amazing than traveling alone or with a partner. They chose a date, time and place to meet in six months and would be conversing like normal until then as they would be lifelong friends.

Morning came and they had breakfast and started

gathering their stuff to head home. Lot's more "BE CAREFUL" remarks were said, be safe and take care of yourselves. Hug and handshakes were handed out and they all set off on their respective paths home.

Once all the hustle and bustle was over, Tom all of a sudden felt very alone. He had lots of friends and he could go anywhere he wanted in the world and in any time or era he wanted to go, but he honestly could only think of one thing and that was his neighbor, Agnes Carnes. She was delightful to talk to and he truly enjoyed her company. He decided he'd brew some tea and take it and a couple of the muffins he'd made over and see how she was faring.

She was delighted to see him and thanked him for bringing brunch, but told him it was unnecessary, she could have put a kettle on.

They talked for about three hours about their lives and the neighborhood and what her aspirations were for the future—she didn't really have much to look forward too, just surviving until it was her time to go home. Was there anything on her bucket list she'd never gotten to accomplish? He'd asked her. She smiled and began to tell him about the love of her life. His name was Frank and they loved each other dearly. They'd had a lot of good times together and had five babies and a lot of grandchildren, but no one seemed to have time for her any more. She probably wouldn't recognize any of them if they walked right up to her. But back to her and Frank. He treated her like a queen and never raised his voice or got upset over anything she or anyone else might have done. He was kind, compassionate and cared about everyone. He was one of a kind. They had never got to travel in their lives, did well to just make a living and raise their children and feed half the neighbor kids. She said they had always wanted to see the ocean. Nothing extravagant, but just to go look at it and enjoy first-hand the amazing work and expanse of it all. Other than that, they had enjoyed a good life full of love for God, family and country. There was always laughter and plenty of food and good times. It was a different time back then when they were raising their kids, people were not afraid of being outside after dark. They talked to their neighbors and helped one another out if and when they needed. You could let your children play unsupervised outside all day with no worries. The doors were never locked and no one would think of taking anything that wasn't theirs. People had respect for one another and themselves.

It's not so much like that anymore, she told him. "I think I've outlived my usefulness." She confessed. "You are definitely here for a reason and I'd like to pursue that with you if you don't mind."

He told her how there were lots of children who could use a tutor and teachers in their local schools who could use volunteers to read to the children, assist with the parties and such. Most parents had to work and couldn't do the volunteer work like they used to. He explained that her Expertise with teaching would be invaluable to some teachers and the kids they were teaching. Kids trust old people, they know they're real and not lying to them or going to promise something they are not going to follow through with.

He knew a couple of the teachers in a school just a couple blocks away that would jump at the chance, and they'd work things around when she could be there. It would give her something to do and she'd make a lot of new friends. Loyal ones, loving ones, caring ones, like only children can honestly be.

She liked the idea and said it would give her a purpose and something worthwhile to do for some of her time. He made a couple phone calls and everything was set up. The teachers were excited and Agnes was too. She then asked Tom about his life.

He explained that he hadn't shared his story with too many people and the handful that had known him for most of his life were the only ones who really knew him. Most thought he was widowed, but truth be known, he'd never been married. He'd loved only one woman in his life and she was killed in a terrible car accident very shortly after they'd gotten engaged. He just didn't have any interest in women after that. He'd had enough hurt to last a lifetime and didn't even want to think about it. He delved into his work and didn't look up for about three years. Then he took some time to grieve and close that part of his life. He was ok then and relatively happy in his work. He probably wouldn't have been a good husband to her anyway as work always seemed to come first. He had always wanted to be a scientist from his youth and his mother had encouraged him in it. He did have a very high IQ and wanted to change the world. You know, make it a better place for everyone, not just the few who could afford anything they needed to enjoy life and take care of themselves. His real passion was time travel. He told her that he had done something and would like to share it with her, but it was imperative that it remain a secret. She couldn't write it in her books, talk about it, or acknowledge she knew anything about it if ever asked. She agreed and he told her he'd achieved it, time travel. Well of course she couldn't believe it but he told her it was true and asked if he could have the honor of showing her the ocean since her husband never got to. When she finished wiping the tears from her eyes, she said she'd love to see it but wasn't really up to a long trip. She explained she got around pretty good in town, but her old bones just wouldn't let her travel that far. Tom smiled and explained he wanted her to experience time travel with him to see the ocean and he'd take her to three or four oceans if she wanted to see them. They could go at sunrise, sunset, and in the middle of the day as well. He assured her it was safe and she would be well rested when she returned. She tentatively agreed and he told her to put on her pedal pushers, grab a hat and a sweater, just in case it was cool and they'd be off. "Just like that? Now?" she asked and Tom smiled again and said "Yes, just like that and definitely now." She got ready and he took her by the hand and entered the coordinates. She took a deep breath, closed her eyes and opened them three seconds later and stood looking at the Atlantic Ocean at sunrise. She stood just staring with tears running down her face. "Oh, Tom, you have done it and Frank would have loved the ocean. Thank you for bringing me." "Let's walk a little on the sand, you want to walk barefoot?" he asked. She giggled and nodded her head. They spent a couple hours there and she soaked in every minute of it. Then he took her on to the Pacific Ocean at sunset, in Hawaii. The palm trees were swaying and they could hear the Hawaiian music from the luau nearby. It was a beautiful sunset and they just sat and watched it slowly slide into the ocean. Tom took her to China to see the Indian Ocean at noon. He got them some lunch and they ate on the beach, then they went home at exactly the time they left. She asked if she'd dreamed it all when she looked at the clock. Tom explained how it worked and thanked her for sharing it with him. Other than his team, no one knew about it and it was something he desperately wanted to tell everyone, but knew he couldn't due to the fact that governments would take it and destroy the whole planet. She thanked him again that he did this for her and promised to never tell anyone as she agreed it was too dangerous for the world. He also told her of the part she'd played in clearing his name and in keeping his friends from being implicated, thus assuring her if that was the only useful thing she'd done in the last twenty years, then her life had great meaning. She may have saved the world.

Tom left smiling and knew exactly what he wanted to do with the rest of his life. He wanted to find someone to share his secret and travel with him the rest of his days. She'd need to be adventurous, untraceable, younger than him, but not necessarily a whole lot. He had it! The perfect woman and according to the best studies he'd found, she would have died on the island of Nikumaroro. If he was wrong and that's not where she was in 1937, then nothing would be lost, but if she were there, he believed he might have found the woman of his dreams. He found the coordinates and left immediately. He arrived the day after her plane was lost to look for her and he found her.

He introduced himself and explained what had happened and where he was from. He also explained that if she went with him, she could never tell who she was, except to his team and of course Mrs. Carnes. They, and now she, were the only people who knew they had achieved time travel. He would make it worth her while and they would have adventures untold if she only would say yes. It didn't take her long to agree and her partner said he felt lucky not to have died already so he would live out his days there on the island knowing he was not going to be rescued; yet resigned to the fact that she would be happy and safe for many years.

So they bid him good bye and Amelia came home with Tom to begin more amazing journeys than she could ever imagine. She was anxious to meet Tom's friends and tell them her story as well as hear theirs.

Tom called them all and asked them to meet at their usual place for dinner, it was imperative he show them something. They knew the meeting place and were pretty anxious to see what Tom had to show them as he seemed so excited on the phone. They met at the designated coordinates at the pre-arranged time and as soon as they arrived, Tom gave them new coordinates to go see what he had to show them. He'd reserved a private table in a very nice restaurant in Paris. They were very impressed. Denver broke the silence after they were seated. "OK Tom, what do you have to show us?" At that cue she walked in the room and Tom stepped to her side. "My friends I want to introduce you to my new consort, friend and maybe my wife. We haven't worked out the details yet; but

I wanted you to meet her. Denver, Margaret, Alan, George, Alison, Steven, Ryan and Jody I'd like to introduce you to my newest friend and confidant, Amelia Earhart."

Eyes flew open and mouths dropped open as well. They couldn't believe it. It was a very silent few seconds before Alison spoke up and said "It's nice to meet you Ms. Earhart. I guess we now know where you disappeared to all those years ago."

She smiled, sat down and proceeded to tell them about her flight and how Tom had found her, told her of her eminent demise and lack of rescue. How she was a hero and one of the most famous people ever to have lived and then had convinced her she could have unlimited adventures for many more years if she'd come and share them with him. "So here I am and it's nice to meet you all as well. Now let's have dinner, shall we?"

Thank you so much for reading my novel. I hope you enjoyed it.

I would appreciate it if you would kindly leave a review on any or all of the below sites:
Amazon.com   or Goodreads.com
Author Kathy Roberts on Facebook

It helps others know if it's something they'd like to read or not; plus your feedback will help me improve as a writer.

I love hearing your thoughts and comments as well. You are the reason we writers write!

You might also enjoy my other books:
"Scars of the Heart" and **"Truth Heals the Heart"** (the sequel, but both are stand-alone books). These novels were set in medieval/Renaissance times, with lots of mystery, murder, espionage, treason and of course romance.

I've also written a paranormal **"The Elevator"** where Samantha is trapped in an elevator by something or someone until she can free 500 souls and find someone to take her place.

All my books can be purchased on Amazon.com in paperback or e-book. I also sell from my website if you'd like autographed copies.
Https://www.authorkathyroberts.weebly.com

Contact me with questions or orders any time at kathyr121@live.com with one of my book titles in the subject line so I know it's not spam.
                                      Kathy

Made in the USA
Columbia, SC
16 June 2023